Geoffrey Foose is the author of *The Leap Forward*, *The Skilled Nut House*, and *Finding Love*. Born and raised in Florida, Geoffrey attended the University of Central Florida, where he earned a degree in psychology. His passion for writing developed during his time at the university. Geoffrey has three children: Kasey, Caitlyn, and Cameron, and he currently lives in Jacksonville, Florida.

I would like to dedicate this book to my children: Kasey, Caitlyn, and Cameron.

Geoffrey Foose

# THE FOUR ACES

AUSTIN MACAULEY PUBLISHERS™

LONDON • CAMBRIDGE • NEW YORK • SHARJAH

**Ordering Information**
Quantity sales: Special discounts are available on quantity purchases by corporations, associations, and others. For details, contact the publisher at the address below.

**Publisher's Cataloguing-in-Publication data**
Foose, Geoffrey
The Four Aces

ISBN 9781647508302 (Paperback)
ISBN 9781647508319 (ePub e-book)

Library of Congress Control Number: 2021919606

www.austinmacauley.com/us

First Published 2021
Austin Macauley Publishers LLC
40 Wall Street, 33rd Floor, Suite 3302
New York, NY 10005
USA

mail-usa@austinmacauley.com
+1 (646) 5125767

I would like to express my deepest appreciation to the following individuals:

Pamela Foose: Thank you for always supporting me. You have taught that if I work on my goals, then my dreams will become possible.

Casey Ratchford: Thank you for your continuous friendship and support. Your creativity and vision have brought this story to life through your incredible illustration.

# Introduction

Since the dawn of time, there has been both good and evil in the world. Most people stay too occupied even to notice. The Lord and his angels continuously watch over and guide God's children every day, while the devil and his demons bring forth darkness and despair upon the earth. Every generation, the mighty archangels instill supernatural powers to one chosen individual they find to be worthy because they cannot fight and stop the evil alone. The devil uses his army of demons, aka the lost souls and creates walking dead creatures called Cryptids. The angels counter by creating Lobos to battle the undead, but they lose more battles than they win. When the angels discover that one worthy individual is not enough, they make a conscious decision to select three additional humans. Michael, the head archangel, chose to call these recruits the Aces. It was now up to Michael and the other archangels to find the right individuals for the job with the hope that they will learn to become a functioning unit.

Michael instructed the other archangels to go out into the world and search for three recruits, while he went looking for the 'one' that would lead them. Archangel Raphael went to Spain while Archangel Gabriel traveled throughout the countries of Asia. Uriel, the last archangel, headed out to the west coast, hoping to find someone worthy. Michael already knew the individual he wanted to lead the Aces; he just needed to travel to Williamsburg, Virginia, first to meet him. He chose this individual because he genuinely had a heart of gold, and no matter what, he always put the needs of others before himself. His name was Micah Ray, and he had no idea that he was about to be recruited by a heavenly archangel.

Michael's presence blinded Micah as he approached him. The angel asked the young man to not be afraid, for he was sent by God to request his assistance. Feeling extremely confused, he said, "I'm just a man, how can I possibly help?"

"Come with me, and I will show you," said Michael.

Having nothing to lose, Micah held out his hand toward the light as the two were transported to Central Park in New York City. They would soon be joined by the other archangels and their chosen recruits. The other three gentlemen selected were named Arthur, Zhang, and Liam, who all looked just as confused as Micah. The angels took human form as they sat down next to the guys, and then began to tell them their plan. After listening to the archangels, Liam and Zhang thought everything sounded great and couldn't wait to become superheroes. Arthur, on the other hand, asked how much money they would be receiving once their mission was over. Micah just shook his head as he began to walk away, telling the angels that he wanted nothing to do with them.

Turning around, he said, "Have fun with the other stooges, if these individuals are our only hope, then we are definitely in trouble." Micah didn't feel it was right for the other guys to say it's awesome to help others, and he had zero respect for Arthur. He thought humans should generally want to help others regardless of recognition, out of the goodness of their heart.

# Chapter 1

Micah walked through the park and up toward the city. He was still in disbelief of what had just occurred and had no idea how he was getting home. Micah decided to call his friend Matthew O' Reily and asked him if he could come to pick him up. At first, he said, "Why are you calling me by my legal name? You know good and well. I go by Mack. May I ask where the hell you are and how come you need me to come to get you?"

"Just get in the car. I will attempt to explain everything once you are here. I am in New York City, and I will be staying at the Hilton Garden Inn on 54<sup>th</sup> Street."

Mack replied, "Okay, I am on my way, but you owe me big time for this one."

Mack is the type of guy that everyone would love to have as a friend. Micah had known Mack since they both were in kindergarten. The two of them had been through everything together, from cub scouts to being high school teammates. They were like brothers and one of the few people Micah could always depend on. Mack was the wise one out of the two and knew how to act serious when needed. The two of them were also roommates and attended the same university. They even talked about starting their own business together one day, that is, if they could manage to survive college first.

Meanwhile, Micah called his younger brother Charlie Wade and asked him to tell their mom he wouldn't be coming home this weekend because he needed to see his friend Tommy Pitts so he could work on his car. Charlie was Micah's stepbrother, but they were closer than your typical step siblings. Charlie jokingly said, "Sure, no problem. But I know you are staying the night there because you have the hots for his sister Toby."

He replied, "Whatever man, today has been a very strange day, and I'm trying to put it behind me. I will see you next weekend." He then decided to turn the television on, hoping to find a game to watch while he waited for Mack to arrive.

Later that evening, as Micah was falling asleep, he heard a knock at the door. He got up to open it for who he assumed was Mack when a demon suddenly attacked him. At that very moment, Michael appeared saving Micah and slaying the demon. Seconds later, Mack walked into the room and asked, "What the hell just happened?"

The archangel grabbed him and started to silence his friend. Micah shouted, "Let him go! He is my best friend. He is here to take me home since YOU decided to teleport me here to New York City."

Michael released his friend and said, "We need to go. There is no time to spare."

Micah informed the angel that he was not going anywhere, and if he wanted his help, then he himself would be selecting the individuals, not him. The archangel stated that this was not a popularity contest, and not just anyone is chosen to become an Ace. Micah disagreed and said, "I can't lead a team if I don't trust them. So, if you still want me to assist, then I will choose the other three."

Getting extremely frustrated, Michael replied, "Fine, I assume one of the three is the gentleman standing next to you. If I am correct, then we need to go now and get Charlie and Tommy before we waste any more valuable time." He asked the archangel how he knew about Tommy and his brother. He replied, "I'm an angel I have been watching over you and the people you care about your entire life." Mack just stood there staring at the angel while they were talking, asking Micah to please explain.

He replied, "Let's just go; I will try to explain everything on the way. Michael will teleport us back to Virginia." Mack then asked about his car.

The angel replied, "Don't worry, we will take your car too. But I must warn you, some humans tend to vomit after they teleport for the first time."

As soon as they arrived back in Virginia, Mack vomited. Yelling and screaming, he said, "That was the strangest feeling I have ever experienced." He stated it felt like he had an out-of-body experience, and toward the end, all his cells and molecules came back together again. The three of them first went to see Tommy. As the archangel was explaining everything to him and Mack, Micah called his brother Charlie. He asked him to drive over to Tommy's house because he had something vital to tell him, and it couldn't wait until tomorrow. Once Charlie arrived, his brother asked him to go inside, and his friends would fill him in on the latest news. Michael looked at Micah and said, "Are you sure these guys are capable of saving the world. Mack

14

seems uncertain, Charlie is still a kid, and Tommy seems off to me."

Micah replied, "They will be fine; Tommy is a bit of a hothead, and Charlie, even as a teenager, is probably the most mature out of the three."

The archangel nodded his head as he said, "Okay, you all need to get some rest; your training starts tomorrow morning."

The following day the guys were introduced to the other archangels. They presented each of them with their unique gifts aka special powers. Raphael granted Mack the gift of the four main elements. This meant he would have the ability to control air, earth, fire, and water. He could also turn his arms into metal upon command, which would assist him during battle. Gabriel gave Charlie the ability to teleport and time-travel. If he could see or picture a destination, then he could travel there. Even though he could travel through time, the angel advised against it. The angel warned him that if he time-traveled, the consequences of his actions could create a negative effect on someone close to him. Uriel had the privilege to present Tommy with the power of telepathic abilities and superhuman strength. The archangel told him to use his powers to help warn people of the evils of this world; his power should never be used as a form of mind-control. Finally, Michael appointed Micah with the ability to create force fields and control electricity.

The guys were excited and overwhelmed with their incredible new gifts and were in disbelief over the entire ordeal. The archangels explained that battling demons and cryptids was no easy task. Charlie asked the angels, "What are cryptids, and why are they so dangerous?"

Michael replied, "They are dead humans that no longer have their soul and survive by consuming human or animal blood. They are mindless creatures that will do anything the demons ask of them."

Charlie stood there in shock after hearing what the angel had just told him. He said, "So they are real, live vampires."

The angel stated, "No, vampires are a myth that society has created for those who have encountered a cryptid and lived to tell about it. An individual can only kill cryptids by burning them or cutting off their heads. Most cryptids will kill only animals unless the demons instruct them to go after a human. When you hear on the news about animals or cattle being butchered or slain in the field, you can almost guarantee cryptids killed them." Michael looked at Charlie. "Tell me now, are you ready to handle all of this because if not, you won't survive very long?"

Micah spoke up before Charlie could even answer him back, saying, "Don't worry, I would not have included my brother if he wasn't capable of handling any situation."

Mack was with Gabriel working on controlling water. The angel told him not to concentrate on things like parting the Atlantic Ocean. He informed him to start small and attempt to fill his glass, standing a few feet away from the faucet. After several attempts at getting water everywhere, the angel told him to clear his mind and try again. Mack took a deep breath and envisioned the water running toward him and into the glass. Once he successfully achieved it, he jokingly said, "Okay, now teach me how to control the weather."

The archangel shook his head, "We don't have time for games. I'm trying to teach you how to control the elements, and as of right now you can barely comprehend one of the four. If you are done playing, then we can continue and maybe get to the element of fire by the end of the week." Mack apologized and informed the angel that he would begin taking his training more seriously going forward.

Uriel decided to take Tommy to another location so he could start training him. The archangel began by telling him why he was gifted with the power of telepathic abilities. He explained to Tommy that he needed to sense when people were in trouble so he could help them. Also, so he could tell people to remain calm during dangerous situations. He told him his power should never be used to control people in making them do specific tasks or things against their will. The angel informed him if he ever abused his power, it would begin to change him for the worse. Meanwhile, they had teleported to an abandoned junkyard. The angel stated, "Let's first work on your strength, then I will go back and teach you more about using your mind."

The training started small by Tommy as he picked up tires, batteries, and other minor car parts. Uriel then asked him to punch the side of a car as hard as he could and then lift it. Tommy was amazed and in shock that he could do these things. The angel then asked him if he was ready for the next step. He replied, "Sure, bring it on. What would you like me to do next, pick up a bus?" He shook his head no as he hurled a school bus at him. Tommy dove on the ground, yelling, "What the hell, are you trying to kill me?"

Uriel instructed him to get up and focus on his voice. The angel said, "Regardless of the size or weight of an object, you have to believe you are strong enough to handle it, or you will fail. Now let's try that again." And he tossed another bus at him. This time not only did he catch the bus, but he threw it as if it was a football over several yards. The archangel praised Tommy telling him that his training was over for the day, but to be prepared for more training in the morning.

Over the next couple of days, Mack had learned to control water and fire and was working on understanding the earth. His ability to manage the winds would come once he mastered everything else. Charlie was having fun teleporting to different areas of the world but did not understand how his powers could benefit the team. Gabriel informed Charlie that if there was ever any danger regardless of where it was, then he would be the one to get the team to that location. The archangel was hoping that one day Charlie would have the mental capacity to teleport demons straight to hell. There was a slim chance that he would become strong enough even though no other Ace in history had ever been successful.

Tommy slowly began to learn how to use his telepathic abilities. He thought the archangel was holding him back and was starting to get frustrated. Uriel did not want Tommy to get too comfortable with his powers; he felt that if he didn't learn to appreciate his powers, then he could start abusing them.

Meanwhile, Mack was finally learning how to control and maintain the wind. One useful thing that Raphael taught Mack was the ability to pull the available air out of an area. He asked the angel why he would need to eliminate the available oxygen from a room, worried it would kill the individuals in the room. The angel replied, "No, not if they are possessed. Humans need oxygen to survive, and demons need their host to be alive. If the host can't breathe, then the demon will abandon the host, and the human will live. If you attempt to kill a demon while it possesses someone, then both parties will die." Seeing him get completely overwhelmed, Raphael promised Mack that it would all begin to make sense to him eventually.

Micah began to learn how to control and utilize his powers. Michael told him, "Concentration is the key because, without focus, your powers would be useless. Over time, you will be able to create force fields for yourself and others when danger is approaching. A lack of concentration can be the difference between life and death. The sole purpose of both cryptids and demons is to trick an individual, harm, or even kill them. When you eventually find yourself in battles, not only will you need to create a shield for you but the other Aces as well." He further added, "The goal should be to not only master your abilities, but learn how to combine and build off each other's strengths. The stronger your team becomes, the easier it will be to defeat your enemy." The archangel told Micah that he would teach him how to control electrical currents and shoot lightning from his hands once everyone had completed their training.

Micah smiled and said, "Sounds good to me, but don't you feel we need to keep our identity a secret from the rest of the world."

Michael replied, "I will leave that up to you."

# Chapter 2

The training continued for several weeks as they were all starting to come together as a team. The archangels pushed Aces to their limits, and each of the guys was beginning to understand the importance of it all. Michael informed the Aces that once their training was complete, he would start to test them against the cryptids. He made it very clear to the guys, "If you are unable to defeat a cryptid, then you will lose if you go up against a demon."

Meanwhile, Michael sent Gabriel to the Blue Ridge Mountains so he could request a meeting with Delisle, Alpha of the Lobos. The Lobos were created for war, but their goal was to live in peace. The archangels needed to know once the war started, if they would be standing next to them ready and prepared to fight. As the day was ending, the angels asked them to take turns pairing together so they could learn how to combine their abilities when needed.

The following week, as Raphael and Uriel were training with the Aces, Michael went on a road trip with Micah. The archangel kept driving through the countryside until it started to rain. He told Micah to get out of the car because he needed to feel the electricity in the air. Michael asked him to concentrate and pull lightning from the atmosphere.

Micah tried for several minutes until he was finally successful. Once he felt the electricity in his hand, he was instructed by the angel to throw it at the stop sign and then try it again by firing it toward the bush. The lightning put a hole through the middle of the sign and caught the bush on fire.

As the rain put the fire out, he asked Micah to abstract electricity from the power line along the road. He did, and this time when he threw it, he was able to blow the stop sign up. Michael said, "Okay, I think you comprehended this notion faster than I was first anticipating. There is one last task to tackle before we head back." Michael picked up the stop sign and threw it at Micah, hoping he would be fast enough to block it. He threw his hands forward and created a force field, stopping the sign seconds before it hit him in the chest.

Elsewhere, Raphael had finally arrived at the Lobo camp and immediately requested to speak to Delisle. The other Lobos formed a barrier around the angel, stating that he was not welcome here. The angel said, "I am just looking to have a peaceful conversation with the alpha leader. I understand you are angry and probably hate angels, but this is bigger than you and me."

Before Raphael could say another word, he heard Delisle say, "Let him through I will hear him out." All the Lobos moved aside and allowed the archangel to pass through to his chambers. The alpha informed the archangel that he had exactly five minutes to explain himself before the elders escorted him out. Raphael pulled up a seat and told him that they were training, not just one recruit, but this time Michael felt it would be beneficial to appoint four new

Aces. Delisle looked at Raphael and said, "So you are putting even more human lives in harm's way. I know our sole purpose is to help angels fight demons and cryptids, but how many of my brothers do I have to lose? Unless my people are purposely attacked, we will not be getting involved in your battles."

As the angel was leaving, he thanked Delisle for his time and wished him well.

As their training came to an end, Michael asked the guys how they felt and if they had any questions. Mack replied, "Questions…I'm still in disbelief over this entire ordeal. I mean, I have always believed in angels and demons, but I never imagined I would ever see one."

Charlie asked the archangels how involved they would be once the fighting began. Michael replied, "We will be fighting next to you, but we only kill demons. Cryptids were once human, which means we are not allowed to kill them. Angels were designed by God to help and assist humans, not to cause them harm."

Tommy chimed in and asked, "Can an archangel die or be killed?"

Michael replied, "God can create or destroy anything, but the All-Mighty would never kill one of us. If anything, he would cast us out from heaven and into hell as he did to Lucifer."

Gabriel added that only an archangel could kill another archangel, which has never occurred and hopefully never will. Michael gave Gabriel a look as if he had no business disclosing that information to the guys.

Micah changed the subject by saying, "Well, if we are done with our training, then it is time for us to head back. I am sure one of you will contact us when we are needed." He turned to his brother and told him it was time for them to return home.

Once they arrived home, the guys were back in their regular routines. Charlie returned to school, asking himself if he would have time to play baseball this season. He loved playing and was a key member of the team; not only was he their starting catcher, but he was also the captain of the squad. He kept remembering his brother telling him that even with their new abilities, it didn't mean we had to change our lives. Which was a silly notion, but Charlie understood that Micah was just trying to keep him and the rest of the team grounded. He enjoyed high school, but he was ready to graduate come June. Charlie planned on attending college if he received a baseball scholarship; if not, then he told his parents he would enlist into the Air Force.

Micah and Mack returned to work and continued with their college courses at night. The two of them talked about starting up their own business together, but that was before their lives became chaotic, thanks to the archangels. Mack asked Micah if he was ready and knew what to do if they encounter a cryptid or demon.

He replied, "Hell no, I am not ready. My only goal would be to stay alive and kill them before they kill me."

He asked Micah another question. "What do we do if one of us gets bit by a cryptid or possessed by a demon?"

Micah looked at Mack, saying, "Well, let's hope that never happens. And besides, did Raphael not tell you? Demons can't possess us because the angels appointed us; I guess he forgot to tell you before he left for the Blue Ridge Mountains."

His friend looked at him and said, "Well, thanks for telling me, now I am only half petrified."

"Come on, man, let's just concentrate on things we have control of, which right now would be passing our business exam later tonight."

The first thing Tommy did once he returned home was check on his sister Toby then he went next story to visit his friend Derek Stokes. Derek was one of Tommy's closest friends, but he despised his friend Micah. Derek lived next to his friend, whereas Micah lived on the other side. Tommy knew at times that his friend did some questionable things; however, he always stood beside him despite his life choices. He felt sorry for Derek because he had an absent mother, and his father and brother would physically abuse him when they consumed too much alcohol. The two of them had been neighbors since birth, and if it weren't for Tommy, Derek would most likely be in prison. Tommy wasn't perfect by any means, and if it weren't for Micah, he most likely would've been just like Derek. Tommy tolerated a lot of things from his neighbor, but the two things Derek was not allowed to do was disrespect or go on a date with Toby.

Derek's hatred for Micah was more than just his friendship with Tommy. He also hated him because Toby had feelings for Micah and wanted nothing to do with him. He worked at the shop with Tommy until he was fired for stealing money from the registrar. Tommy pleaded with his boss to give his friend another chance, but his boss told him that it was a hard no. Derek kept asking his friend where he had been for the past few days, and Tommy kept saying he had something come up last minute. Derek wouldn't leave the issue alone, and Tommy finally cracked and told him about his training. He told his friend that he had special powers, and an archangel was training him.

His friend's first response was, "Bullshit! You are pulling my leg. Why are you lying to me with such a crazy story?"

Tommy lifted his car with one hand to prove that he was telling the truth. He asked what other powers he possessed, and Tommy replied, "That is all for now."

Derek just stared at him saying, "Damn, you are a real, live Superman. Do you have any weaknesses?"

He just shook his head and said, "No, I don't believe so, but please keep this to yourself. This is not supposed to be public knowledge. I'm sure Uriel and the other archangels will strip me of my powers if they find out."

Later that evening, Micah came home to see his mom and stepdad. Micah lost his biological father due to a brain tumor when he was only two. His mother met and married Charlie's dad a year later. Charlie's dad was a commanding officer in the Navy and took excellent care of their mom. His mom taught a couple of college courses each semester so that she wouldn't get bored. Mrs. Wade preferred to stay home and take care of her family. There was nothing she loved more than her two sons. Mrs. Wade was pleased that her sons loved and supported each other. She would tell her friends all the time how lucky she was and how she couldn't be any prouder of her boys.

As the guys were getting accustomed to being superheroes, the archangels returned to heaven. The angels understood why Michael decided to have four Aces instead of just one. They knew the world wasn't getting any better, but worried what God thought of Michael's actions. Being the hierarchy, Michael asked to speak with God, and as always, God granted his request. Before Michael could even say a word, God informed him that he must take full responsibility for his decisions. If he felt that it was necessary to appoint four individuals instead of the traditional one, then that would fall entirely on him. God stated that His children would always have a choice in life, but His angels' only obligation was to serve Him and watch over His children. Michael acknowledged God as he walked away and left His presence.

Michael left to find his fellow angels to tell them that God was pleased with his decision regarding the Aces. Once he saw them, he noticed that each of them looked troubled. He asked each archangel why they had a look of concern on their face. Raphael said, "I feel Mack is a lot like Micah, but he plays too much. And I worry when things get real, will he be ready to fight?"

Gabriel chimed in, saying, "Charlie is a great kid, but he is still in high school. I know when he is with the others, he will be protected. But is he mentally strong enough to make the important decisions when he is standing alone?"

Uriel just stared at Michael and said, "You already know I have concerns regarding Tommy. We may have given him too much power, but I hope I'm wrong."

Michael told the angels he had concerns too with Micah selecting the other Aces, but he trusts that he made the right choice. The only thing we can do for them now is to guide them and continue providing support when needed.

# Chapter 3

Back in the pits of hell, the demons were busy planning and plotting their first move. They knew the archangels were recruiting a new Ace but laughed uncontrollably when they heard they broke tradition and recruited not just one but four individuals. While the demons were laughing and joking, Ashmead, Lucifer's first-in-command, appeared. He instructed his minions to shut up and listen. He said, "Even though the Lobos are neutral right now and these recruits are young, remember who is training them. I didn't survive all the trials that Lucifer put me through to stand pat. The recruits and I were all trained by an archangel."

One of the demons interrupted Ashmead and said, "Boss, you know the devil doesn't like when you refer to him as an archangel; he is the ruler of hell."

He turned to him with a furious look and said, "Don't ever interrupt me again." He then destroyed him with only a snap of his finger. Ash, as the devil called him, instructed the demons to prepare the cryptids for battle. "We need to attack soon while the Aces are still experimenting with their new abilities."

Meanwhile, the cryptids were terrorizing humans along the east coast while also feeding on any livestock they encountered. Cryptids will only kill or turn a human if they are instructed by a demon or ordered by Madame Isabelle. Ashmead turned Isabelle because he took a liking to her and couldn't bear his life without her. She despised him to this very day for turning her and killing her unborn child but was always too afraid ever to challenge him. She felt trapped because one day she was planning to start a family with the man of her dreams and then the very next, she became one of the undead. Ashmead killed her husband and turned her into a cryptid. Even though it had been two centuries since that had occurred, Isabelle remained hopeful that one day she would have her revenge.

Elsewhere, the Lobos were getting concerned about all the activity the cryptids were creating along the coastline. Delisle was always observing trying to determine if they were hunting and feeding or if they were stirring up trouble. The Alpha's son Adrian was urging his father to get the pack together so they could attack the cryptids while they were small in number. He said, "Father, they are loose and reckless, and the demons are not with them. We need to attack now while we have the opportunity."

His father replied, "Our people only fight when threatened. And right now, the cryptids are not targeting us."

Adrian being extremely frustrated said, "I don't agree with your leadership skills. You would rather wait until something happens and then possibly experience more of our people perishing along the way."

Having heard enough from his son, he cast him from the pack and told him not to return until he was ready to follow his lead. Adrian looked at his father as he told him he would handle the cryptids himself.

Adrian decided to meet these new Aces for himself. He was hoping that if his father wouldn't help him, then maybe they would be more of assistance. He overheard Raphael talking to his father about the new Aces and how there was a war coming soon. Adrian did not know how the Aces felt, but he was tired of being a pawn to this never-ending war between good and evil. He wondered if he could talk to the lead Ace, then maybe he would listen. He knew the angels wouldn't listen to him because, in Michael's eyes, the Lobos were nothing more than expendable creatures at his despair. His only goal right now was to find Micah and kill as many cryptids along the way.

Back in Virginia, Micah and Mack were heading to campus to study for their exam. As Micah was walking through the courtyard, he saw Derek and Toby. He walked over and hugged Toby and asked her how she was doing. Micah jokingly wondered if Derek was bothering her. She smiled, saying, "No, he is innocent. He knows we are just friends, but that doesn't mean he won't try to flirt every chance he gets."

He replied, "Derek knows he better be nice to you, or he will have to deal with your brother and me."

Toby laughed and asked him if he would be interested in going to a play with her on Friday night.

Micah replied, "Sure, text me the details; I have to run, my class is starting soon."

As Toby kissed him on the cheek, he saw Derek give him a dirty look from the corner of his eye.

As the guys were taking their exams, two cryptids decided to visit Charlie. As soon as Charlie walked into his house, he was attacked by them. He quickly kicked one of them off him and teleported to Tommy's house, hoping that he would be there. Charlie suddenly appeared in his bedroom startling him. Before Tommy could even react, he saw why he had teleported to his house. He shouted, "Charlie lookout!" as he punched one of the creatures in the jaw. They were able to run into the living room where Tommy grabbed one of the cryptids by the throat and threw him directly into the fireplace. Charlie grabbed the fire iron and stabbed the other one in the back, right before Tommy took the ax from the closet and cut his head off. He looked at Charlie and said, "Looks like the demons are handing out orders, and we are at the top of their list. Let's go find Mack and Micah and make sure they are okay."

Once they arrived at the campus, they saw Mack walking to the parking lot. Tommy yelled out to him and asked him if Micah was still there. Mack turned around, walking toward the guys saying, "He left about ten minutes before I finished my exam. I assumed Micah left and went home, but I see that his car is still here." He asked the guys what was going on and if they thought Micah was in danger.

Charlie blurted out in a frantic tone, "Dude, cryptids were at my house waiting for me once I arrived home. Luckily for me, Tommy was back and helped me kill the evil bastards."

Mack asked, "Do you think one of them has Micah?"

Tommy replied, "I hope not, but let's divide up and search the campus. He will turn up eventually; he has to for our sake."

Minutes before they arrived at the campus, Micah was approached by a beautiful woman. She told him not to be afraid because she wasn't there to hurt him.

He glanced at her saying, "Are you a demon or a cryptid, and why should I not be worried if you are one?"

She told him that her name was Isabelle, and she was a cryptid but hated the demons more than he did.

Micah replied, "So, are you telling me that you obey them every time they give you an order?"

She just shook her head and said, "What other choice do I have? We all feel like prisoners to the demons. We attack the Lobos and other humans out of fear, not a necessity. I have never hurt or attacked another human in my life; you can believe me or not, but that's the truth. Please think about what I just told you."

Micah put his head down, and when he looked up again, she was gone. Hearing his friend's voices calling out for him, he decided to walk back toward the parking lot.

As Micah approached the other Aces, his brother ran to him and asked if he was okay. He ensured everyone that he was just fine and had decided to take a walk around the campus while Mack was finishing his exam. Tommy said, "I'm glad you are fine, but we have a problem. Your brother and I were just attacked by two cryptids which we killed, but I'm sure more are coming this way."

Micah suggested they all stay with him at his apartment.

Tommy replied, "Okay, I will go with your brother so we can both grab some of our personal belongings."

"Sounds good," said Micah. "Me and Mack will go ahead to the apartment, and then we can begin to sort everything out."

When they arrived at the apartment, Michael was there waiting on Micah. He asked if Charlie and Tommy were safe.

Micah got into Michael's face saying, "Yes, they are fine, thank you for asking. Where have you and the other angels been?"

"We were in heaven. We can only stay on Earth for so long at any given time. Why do you think we created the Aces?"

Micah replied, "I thought it was to boost your ego."

"ENOUGH!" said Michael. "I came here because I feel the demons are planning something sooner rather than later. There will be even more cryptids coming, I'm sure."

Mack asked Michael, "What happens if next time the demons are with the cryptids?"

The archangel replied, "Then the angels and I will be ready. Your powers can only slow down a demon; the only way to kill one is with a holy dagger. It is the weapon of every archangel. Once Tommy, Charlie, and the other angels arrive, we will develop a strategy in case they decide to attack in greater numbers."

# Chapter 4

The guys and the other three angels arrived within minutes of each other. Michael told the Aces that he and the other archangels would be around watching the surrounding areas. He promised to return if the demons appeared with the cryptids. Micah blurted out, "I don't think all cryptids are here to harm us." He stated that they might attack because they are scared and don't want the demons to destroy them.

All the angels turned their heads, saying, "Don't be stupid or naïve; they are evil."

Micah replied, "You stated that cryptids were once human. So maybe they are scared to disobey the demons. I encountered one today, and she didn't try to hurt me."

Gabriel asked if this woman was tall and skinny with jet black hair.

Micah nodded his head "Yes, how did you know?"

The archangel replied, "The woman you saw was Isabelle. She is the only woman ever to be turned and is in charge of the other cryptids. Don't fall for her tricks, she is playing you."

Micah stood there, saying, "I will make my judgment regarding her."

As the angels turned toward the light and ascended to the heavens, the guys confronted Micah for not telling them about the woman that had approached him. He said, "There is not much to tell. I would rather learn more about her before I jump to conclusions. Maybe she wants the fighting to end as well. It is our duty to collect all the facts; the angels might not have everything right. We have all heard the saying, "The enemy of my enemy is my friend." Isabelle may be an ally and not a threat."

Tommy replied, "You do what you think is best, but if I see a cryptid, I'm going to kill it. Let's all try to get some sleep. I will take first watch."

The following day was Friday and Mrs. Wade was starting to worry about her sons. She called Charlie and asked him if he was going to school. He told his mom that Micah was taking him before he went into work. She asked to talk to her oldest son, so Charlie handed the phone to his brother. She told him that she had a funny feeling that something was wrong. She went on to say, "You are missing work, going to New York, and keeping your brother out on school nights. Are you in some kind of trouble?"

He ensured his mom that everything was fine, and if that changed, then he would call her. He told Charlie and his mom that he would not be at Charlie's game later because he had previous plans. She told both her boys that she loved them very much as she said goodbye.

As Mack and Tommy were on their way to work, Micah found himself driving around after dropping his brother off. He thought about what Isabelle and Gabriel had told him but still wasn't sure what to believe. He knew cryptids and demons were both real, but is it even possible to trust a cryptid? Isabelle may be playing him, or maybe, just maybe, she was telling the truth. He just didn't want to put anyone in harm's way while he figured it out. Micah decided to drive down the east coast while checking the internet for any animal attacks. Cryptids were hard to recognize from afar. He learned by experience that all cryptids are cold to the touch, move extremely fast, plus they all have beaming yellow eyes. So no matter where Micah went, he knew they would not be able to surprise him.

After driving for about an hour, Micah saw two individuals run across the road. The speed they were running at was what ultimately caught his attention. He pulled his car off to the side and decided to follow their trail. He eventually found what he thought were two cryptids fighting, but as he got closer, he noticed one of the individuals was something else. The black individual jumped on the back of the cryptid and ripped its head clean off. Afterward, the individual charged out towards Micah as he put up a force field protecting himself. Micah yelled out, "What are you? I know you are not a cryptid or a demon."

The individual replied, "No, I am neither. My name is Adrian, and I'm second in command of the Lobos. Are you one of the Aces?"

He looked at Adrian and said, "Yes, I am; my name is Micah."

The Lobo asked him to walk with him as they both had a lot to discuss.

Adrian started by telling Micah that he was born a Lobo, and his father was the first to be created by Michael. He told him that his father, Delisle, is a man of peace and does not see eye to eye with the archangels. Throughout the years, hundreds of his people had died protecting the humans from the cryptids. "The worst part is if we are under attack, your precious archangels are never around to help us. It is like the angels only have three objectives: obey God, protect the humans, and kill demons if needed. So you see, the angels are using both of us to fight their battles."

Micah replied, "I can see where you are coming from, but I do feel the angels are here to offer their assistance. Lobos, just like cryptids, are half-human, which means the angels are prohibited from hurting or killing them."

Adrian asked Micah to come with him, and together they would kill all the cryptids. Micah told him that if they waged war, just the two of them, then they would be on the losing end.

Adrian turned around and said, "Fine, I will do this alone as he walked away."

Walking back toward the car, Micah remembered that he had promised Toby that he would accompany her to the play later. As he was driving back, Isabelle appeared in the passenger seat, scaring him in the process. He told her that she couldn't keep creeping up on him whenever she feels like it. She asked him if he had thought about what she told him the last time they talked. He told Isabelle that he didn't trust her as far as he could throw her. He asked, "If you truly want the fighting to stop then why don't you and the other cryptids stop terrorizing the humans and attacking the Lobos?"

She said, "We haven't attacked the Lobos in quite some time, but we have to defend ourselves when the Alpha's son is hunting us. We all should be attacking the demons." She did add that no matter what she does, the majority of the cryptids will probably still follow any orders given by Ashmead. She leaned over and kissed him on the cheek, telling him that he reminded her of her husband. Right before she vanished, she said, "See if I wanted to bite you I would have, you need to get faster at using your powers. Any other cryptid would have bit you before you even had a chance to react."

On the way back to town, Micah called Charlie and wished him good luck for his game later. He then checked in with Mack and Tommy to make sure there were no other cryptid attacks. Mack said, "It has been a very calm day even though our boss was pissed off at you for calling out."

He replied, "He will get over it, besides why give employees five sick days a year if you don't use them."

Tommy told Micah to be respectful and a gentleman to his sister. He also said he would be attending the play as well, and Mack would be in the stands looking out for Charlie.

He replied, "Okay, sounds good. And don't worry, I'm always respectful to Toby."

"Of course, you are," Tommy said. "But will you ever admit that you are crazy about her? My sister doesn't hide her feelings, why should you?"

As Micah ended their conversation, he told Tommy he would tell him about his day later.

Micah drove straight home to shower and changed before heading over to pick up Toby for the evening. He felt that he should wear something business-casual as he laid a pair of black slacks and a red dress shirt on his bed. He kept telling himself that tonight was not a date, but Micah couldn't deny that he did have feelings for her. He continuously asked himself, *is it wise to date your best friend's sister?* He felt if he did and things went south, it would ruin his relationship with both of them. He couldn't think about that right now; he just wanted to get dressed and arrive at the play on time. No one wants to be late to a play. Micah grabbed his wallet along with his keys as he walked out the front door.

A few minutes later, Micah arrived to pick up Toby. She came to the door wearing a black dress with her hair down and curled. He said, "Wow, you look gorgeous this evening."

Toby replied, "You clean up very nice yourself, sir."

He asked her, "Should we be on our way?"

Smiling, she laid her hand on his arm saying, "Of course, we don't want to be late, and besides, I want a seat close to the front." As Toby got into the car, Tommy told him to be careful, and that he will meet them there.

As they were driving to the theater, Toby surprised Micah by asking if he had feelings for her. He replied, "It's complicated! There are a lot of things happening in my life right now plus your brother is my best friend."

She turned her head in disgust, saying, "That has to be the most pathetic answer I have ever heard. It was a yes or no question, and you crapped all over it, forget I even asked."

He attempted to keep explaining himself, but at that point, she quit listening to him. When they arrived, he asked if they could start over because he didn't want one question to ruin their entire evening. He told Toby that he did care about her more than she will ever know.

She looked at Micah and said, "If that is true, then why don't you kiss me?" He then got out of the car and walked around to open her door. As he held out his hand to help her out, he brought her close to him and kissed her. She smiled and said, "See, was that so hard to do?" as they kissed each other again.

Once they walked into the auditorium, they were greeted by a familiar face. Derek was standing by the ticket stand and headed toward Toby as soon as he spotted her. He said with an angry voice, "What the hell Toby, you tell me no but decide to show up with this punk instead?"

Micah got between Derek and Toby and asked him to go home before he did something he would regret. Derek yelled at Micah, telling him that he took Tommy from him and now Toby.

She replied, "For the last time, I am not your girl and never will be. Please go home, you are drunk."

He went to throw a punch at Micah, who then shielded himself by using his powers. Derek bent over in pain, yelling, "What did you do? I think my hand is broken."

Toby stood there confused because he didn't hit anything when he threw his punch. A few seconds later, Tommy arrived and pulled Derek to the side. He asked what was going on, and his sister replied, "Nothing I can't handle, but it's probably best if he leaves." He walked his friend to the curb and told him he needed to go home. Toby grabbed Micah's hand as they walked to their seats. She looked at him, saying, "I don't know what just happened, but I hope you explain it to me later." He kissed her hand as he promised to tell her eventually.

Feeling bad for his friend, Tommy decided to help Derek. He caught up with him and offered to take him home, but Derek declined, saying, "Just go watch the play with your real friend. No matter what I do, I will never be good enough for Toby, and you will always think of me as a charity case. So do me a huge favor and just leave me alone."

Tommy, not knowing what to say to his friend, just watched him as he kept walking down the street. Tommy walked back into the auditorium and saw Micah and Toby were holding hands. He decided to sit a few rows behind them, trying to give them some space. Tommy being the protective brother, didn't think anyone was good enough for his sister, but if she was going to date anyone, he was glad it was his friend Micah. After the play was over, Tommy hugged his sister and told Micah that he would meet him at his apartment in about an hour. He told Tommy that sound like a plan as he opened the car door for Toby. She just looked at Micah and said, "An hour, well, that gives you plenty of time to explain to me what happened with Derek's hand."

Pulling into Toby's driveway, Micah said, "Well, as promised, we had an amazing time together. Thank you for asking me to go with you. I couldn't have asked for a prettier date this evening."

Toby just looked at him, saying, "Thank you for the sweet compliment, but you are avoiding my question."

He replied, "It's complicated. I feel if I tell you then you may look at me differently or your life could be in danger."

She replied, "Okay, now you have me worried; I am not getting out of this car until you come clean with me."

He asked if they could make out instead. She gave him a look, "You promised never to hurt me, so if you want to keep that promise, then tell me now."

He took her hand and said, "Okay, here it goes. An archangel named Michael came to me a few weeks ago and asked for my help. He wanted me to be a protector for all humanity and appoint me and three other individuals with supernatural abilities. My superpower is creating a force field, which is what Derek hit when he threw his punch."

Before Micah could say another word, Toby pulled her hand away from him, saying, "Thanks a lot for telling me that ridiculous story, I hate you." She got out of the car and slammed the door. Micah wanted to follow her, but he knew she needed time to cool down and process everything.

While driving back to his apartment, Michael appeared in the car. The first thing he said was, "How dare you to tell her about your abilities? How can we keep humans safe if they start to learn about Aces, angels, demons, and every other creature on Earth? There could be pure chaos and panic among the entire human race."

Micah replied, "I cannot lie to Toby; it would destroy our relationship."

"Well, I hope you are happy; the more you tell her, the more curious she will become. Which could eventually put her into danger because the demons could use her as leverage to get to you and the other Aces."

"Well, if that happens," said Micah. "Then I guess that is where you and the other archangels come in to help us."

"Our primary goal is to protect humans; we don't like to kill demons. It is not in our nature to destroy anything."

Micah gave Michael a very unpleasant look as he told him, "If someone that I care about is in danger, you better destroy whatever is in their path, or I will quit being an Ace. That is a guaranteed promise!"

Michael replied, "Yes, of course, we would never let a demon purposely harm a human in our presence. I'm just asking you to be careful. The fewer humans know about the supernatural, the safer they are."

# Chapter 5

The game was at the top of the ninth when the cryptids began to attack. Charlie threw his catcher mask as he looked for his mom in the stands. As soon as he spotted her, he yelled for Mack to draw them away from the bleachers so he could start saving everyone. Charlie started by teleporting his mom to safety. She was so startled by what was occurring that she became speechless. He looked at his mom and said, "I will explain everything later, but I have to go back and help the others. If not, people will die from the cryptid attacks." Mrs. Wade tried to reply and ask what in the world are cryptids, but she was still in shock. Charlie teleported back to the field and immediately began getting everyone to safety, but first, he put his mask back on so people wouldn't see who was grabbing them. As he was teleporting back and forth, he noticed another creature on the field fighting alongside Mack.

The mystery creature was Adrian, who had been tracking the cryptids. Mack yelled out to him, "I'm guessing you are a Lobo, and I shouldn't worry about you."

He yelled back, "Yes I am. Now shut up and help me kill these bastards. We will exchange pleasantries later." He told Mack, "Don't let them scratch or bite anyone here.

Please make sure to swing your blades at their arms or chest; this will cause them to fall forward, allowing you to chop off their head."

He asked Adrian how he knew about him and his powers. He replied, "My dad is the Alpha, plus I have already met and spoken with your friend Micah. Now please can we focus on killing them and staying alive?" Once everyone was safe, Charlie came and teleported both Adrian and Mack to his brother's apartment.

Once they arrived, the three of them were greeted by Tommy, who was uneasy about having a Lobo in his presence. He felt as long as Adrian was there, they would be in danger of having another cryptid attack. Mack said, "Don't worry, he is cool. The cryptids were not following him; he was tracking them." The Lobo asked where Micah was and when was the last time anyone saw him.

Tommy replied, "About a half-hour ago. He should be on his way. He is taking my sister home."

Charlie asked how the play went, and Tommy just gave him a look, like that's not even important right now. As he was about to apologize to Tommy for his untimely question, the archangels appeared.

"We all need to talk as soon as Micah arrives; Michael believes the demons were planning something terrible and will most likely attack again very soon."

On his way home, Michael appeared and told Micah that there was an attack on the baseball field. He informed him that everyone was fine, and Charlie and Mack were waiting for them back at Micah's place. Micah asked how just the two of them fought off so many cryptids. The archangel replied, "We had help from the Alpha's son.

Adrian is currently on his own solo mission to find and kill the cryptids, which are probably why they retaliated and started attacking humans."

"Where is Adrian now?" Micah asked.

"He is currently at your apartment with your brother."

"Instead of lecturing me, don't you feel that you should have led with that first?"

Michael replied, "Possibly, but now you know. So can we move forward with the issue at hand?"

Once they arrived at the apartment, Tommy asked about his sister. Micah replied, "She is safe, but she has a lot of questions about what happened with Derek. I told her that I was anointed with supernatural powers, so when he threw his punch, the impact of the force field broke his hand. She called me a liar and slammed my car door as she got out."

"Don't worry, she will come around. She likes you too much to stay mad," said Tommy.

Adrian interrupted them, saying, "I do believe we have more pressing issues to deal with besides your girlfriend's emotional state."

Charlie asked who gave the cryptids orders to attack innocent people at the game. Michael stated that only Ashmead and Isabelle could hand out orders to the cryptids.

Mack asked, "What about Lucifer? Doesn't he issue out orders sometimes?"

Raphael replied, "Not really, he mainly focuses on tempting humans to disobey and defy God."

Micah said, "Regardless of who is giving the orders, we must stop them and protect everyone around us. But first, let's make sure our loved ones are safe and out of danger."

While everyone was busy planning their next move, Derek was still stumbling through the city, trying to get home. As he was approaching his neighborhood, someone wearing all black stopped him. Derek was so drunk that he didn't even notice that this particular individual had red eyes. The stranger asked him if he was having a bad day. He looked at the individual thinking, *are you a stupid moron?*

Derek said, "Of course I'm having a bad day. What gave it away, my stumbling down the sidewalk or my fat broken hand? The girl that I love rejected me, my best friend betrayed me, and the person I hate the most somehow broke my hand, and I don't know how he did it. So yes, today has been one of the worst days of my life."

The stranger replied, "What if I told you I could make all the wrongs right. Would you be interested in getting your revenge?"

He asked him, "How can you help make my life better?"

The demon smiled and said, "Let me help you to your house, and I will tell you everything."

As soon as Derek and the stranger walked into the house, his father started yelling at him for missing work. He then asked his son who the individual was walking in with him. Before Derek had an opportunity to reply, the demon sprung toward Mr. Strokes and killed him. Standing there in disbelief, Derek yelled, "You are a demon! Tommy was right; I should have listened to him. What do you want with me? I am no one."

The demon said, "My name is Jason, and I want you to give me permission to use your body as a vessel."

He looked at the demon, saying, "You are asking to possess my body, and you need my permission to do so. The answer is hell no!"

Jason replied, "Okay, I will kill your brother and the young woman you love, and I will do it right in front of you. Your other option is you can say yes and together we will kill Micah and his family."

Derek pleaded with the demon saying, "Please leave them alone I will do whatever you ask."

"So is that a yes? I need to hear you say the words."

Derek replied, "Yes, just leave the people I care about alone."

As soon as the demon possessed Derek, he left his previous vessel lying dead in the middle of the living room.

The first thing the demon did after he took control of Derek, was walk down the hallway and kill his brother, who was asleep in his room. Derek, who was imprisoned within his own body, was helpless as he witnessed his brother's death. He became angry, which only fueled the demon to cause even more destruction. The demon knew that Derek was trapped, and eventually, he would experience so much hate that the two would become one. As the demon prepared to leave, he invaded the kitchen to eat whatever was available. He needed to eat, not to function, but to keep the vessel alive.

Once Jason left the Strokes' house, he started to walk toward Tommy's house. He knocked on the door and asked if Toby was home. Mrs. Pitts answered the door and told Derek no, she was out with her friends. She looked at him, knowing something was wrong and asked him if he was feeling alright. Instead of responding to her question, the demon decided to silence her by putting his arm through her chest, killing her instantly. He then dragged her body to the kitchen as he washed the blood off his body. The demon could hear Derek screaming within asking, "Why are you killing? You promised to leave them alone."

Jason laughed, saying, "You are one stupid human being. I'm a demon, killing and lying is what I do. My job is to tear apart the Aces and show Lucifer that I should be first-in-command, not Ashmead. Now please enjoy the ride. I promise to kill you quickly once I'm done with you."

Back at the apartment, Michael told the Aces that he felt something wasn't right at Tommy's house. Mack asked, "What do you mean you feel…you feel what? We need more information than that." Each of the archangels grabbed one of the guys as they teleported them to their old neighborhood. Micah and Charlie ran over to check on their mother while Tommy watched Derek drive away on his father's motorcycle. He thought it was odd, especially since Mr. Strokes had never allowed his son to ride it. Uriel shouted for Tommy as he discovered his mother's body. As he held his mom in his arms, he called Derek, hoping he heard or saw something as he drove away.

The demon answered the phone using Derek's voice and said, "What's up, buddy, sorry I had to run off without saying hello to you."

Tommy replied, "Did you see anyone come or go at my parents' house? My mom is dead."

Laughing hysterically, he tells Tommy, "Don't worry; I evened it out. I made sure to kill your mom and Derek's entire family. By the way, you can call me Jason." And he ended the call.

He looked up at Uriel with hate in his eyes and said, "Let's go; we have a demon to kill."

Once Micah checked on his mother, he heard Mack calling for him outside. He told Micah that Mrs. Pitts was dead, and they all needed to head over to the Strokes' house because they were dead too. He told Mack and his brother to check the Strokes' house while he went to comfort Tommy. Both homes were destroyed, and the bloodshed was horrifying. Michael told the Aces that they needed to find Tommy's dad and sister, along with Charlie's parents, and get them to a safe place. Tommy said, "My dad is out of town on business, and I'm not sure where my sister went."

Micah took out his cell phone and dialed Toby's number. He tried calling twice, but he got no answer. He finally texted her and wrote, "Please call me; it's about your family." Seconds later, Toby called him back and asked if her family was alright. He asked her where she was and got her location. She told him her friend's address and within seconds Charlie was there to retrieve her.

Charlie appeared so fast it took Toby and her friend by surprise. She asked how he got there so quickly and where his brother was. He told her that everything Micah had told her was true, and if she wanted to stay alive, then she must come with him immediately.

Not knowing what to say, she grabbed her bag and told him, "Okay, let's go, I trust you." Michael ordered Gabriel to stay at Wade's house and keep watch while he sent Uriel to locate Mr. Pitts. He asked the archangels to watch over them and keep them safe. Gabriel then asked if it was wise to split up.

He said, "Raphael and I will stay with the guys until we can track down and stop this rogue demon."

# Chapter 6

Derek, aka the demon, decided to track down Toby at her friend's house. He pulled into the driveway and rang the doorbell. Her friend answered the door, and when she noticed who it was, she slammed the door. The demon kicked the door in and screamed at her telling her not to be so rude. She asked him how did he know Toby was there and how his hand healed so quickly. The demon stared at her with his red eyes and said, "Sweetheart, I'm not Derek, and now you must die. I can't afford for anyone to live after crossing paths with me. I'm sorry, it's not personal; I came here for Toby, not you." After Jason took care of the young lady, he was back on the road. He said to himself I will eventually find Toby, but first, I think I will have some fun.

Meanwhile, back at the apartment, Toby sat on the couch, trying to understand what had happened. She watched a man break his hand without hitting anything, and now she witnessed Charlie appear and teleport her across town. She didn't know what was more surprising; humans with supernatural powers or sitting right in front of an archangel. Micah brought her a glass of water and sat down next to her. He said, "I know all of this is overwhelming, but you are safe now. I still find myself in shock that all of this is even real. Not only do Charlie and I have supernatural powers, but so do Mack and Tommy."

She looked at Micah and got off the couch as she stared at her brother. She slapped Tommy in the face telling him that he had no right to keep this from her. Michael tried to explain that it was for the best to keep her and everyone else in the dark. He said, "Look at what has happened to Derek, as soon as Tommy told him, the demons exploited him. The demons will use people's weaknesses to their advantage. The first ones they target are their friends and family, and then they will attack a person's livelihood, which could be their social status, job, or financial situation?"

She replied, "So what are we waiting for, let's go kill them."

Seconds later, Raphael interrupted Toby by telling everyone that Derek had killed again. Michael asked if it was someone the Aces knew. He replied, "No, it was the young lady that Toby was visiting this evening." She asked the archangel who else had he killed today.

Tommy put his arms around his sister and told her, "The demon known as Jason had now killed four people. He has murdered Derek's father and brother, your friend, and our mother."

Hearing the shocking news, Toby dropped to her knees and burst into tears crying, "NO, not momma too!"

Tommy kneeled on the floor beside his sister as they both continued to cry.

As Micah was planning their next move, Michael could sense someone was approaching the apartment. He asked Mack to open the door and warned him a cryptid was heading this way. He opened the door, and before Mack could do anything, Adrian leaped through the air and pinned the cryptid to the ground. He asked her where the rest of her army was, and if she promised to tell him, then he would kill her last.

Isabelle yelled out, "Someone, please get this mutt off of me; I'm not here to fight." Michael ordered Mack to cut her head off while Adrian had her pinned, but was stopped by Micah. He told everyone to stand down and allow Isabelle to talk. Michael advised against it, telling Micah that they needed to kill her while they had the chance.

Micah stated, "She is completely outnumbered, and if she tries anything stupid, she will be dead. So we all should let her explain herself because she can't be that stupid to walk into a kill zone voluntarily."

As he got off her, Adrian looked at her and said, "Talk. You have exactly three minutes."

Isabelle requested to talk to Micah alone. He replied, "No, not this time. Adrian told you that you had three minutes, so stop wasting our time, you are down to two and a half."

"So you want me to talk to you in front of the other Aces, the archangels, dog-man, and your girlfriend; okay, fine. There is going to be a war among the demons, and the cryptids will most likely die, including me. Ashmead is first in command of Lucifer and the demon that turned me. He likes to control situations and afflict fear among everyone. He mostly hates the angels and cryptids but has never harmed one because he has a sick affection for me. Another demon by the name Jason has always been jealous of Ashmead and is attempting to overthrow him. So he will use any method possible to defeat him that includes killing anything in his path. Can he beat Ashmead? Possibly, who knows, but I don't want to find out because it will get bloody.

"The first thing Jason will do is recruit as many cryptids as possible. If they refuse, he will kill them. The majority of all the cryptids are victims just like me. Most would be completely content to co-exist and feed off of livestock and other small animals for the rest of their lives. If you don't believe me, then ask Micah. If I wanted to cause someone harm, I would have already. Tell your buddies about the kiss we shared and how I told you that your response time was horrible."

Toby replied, "You kissed her, are you kidding me?"

"She kissed me on the cheek," Micah said. "But yes, if she wanted to hurt me, she could have that day." He asked Isabelle directly, "How exactly do you expect us to help?"

She requested that Adrian and one of the Aces come with her to warn as many cryptids as possible. Michael replied, "Absolutely not, it's a trap."

Micah looked at Michael and said, "You appointed me the leader, right? Then let me give the orders. Until Isabelle tries to hurt someone or lies to me, I consider her an ally."

He asked Tommy to go with them, and his response was, "No, I will not leave my sister."

Before Micah could reply, Charlie volunteered to go with Adrian. He looked at his brother and said, "I need to do this; my job is to get people to safety. I can't do that if I remain here."

Micah said, "Okay, but if anything goes wrong, kill her and teleport yourself and Adrian back here immediately."

She looked at Micah and said, "Will you ever trust me, or is that just wishful thinking?"

He replied, "I'm starting to, but I can't make any promises."

The next morning Uriel returned to the apartment with Mr. Pitts. He was not particularly happy about coming with him, as was evident by his yelling and screaming at the angel. All the commotion had awoken everyone from their sound sleep. Toby ran out of the bedroom as soon as she heard her father's voice.

He asked her, "Whose apartment am I in?"

She replied, "It's a long story, but this is Mack's and Micah's apartment."

Tommy came out of the other bedroom and asked his dad to have a seat. He told his dad that things were happening right now that he won't understand. Mr. Pitts looked at his two children and asked about his wife.

Toby said, "Dad, mom is dead; she was killed by a demon who has possessed Derek."

He looked at her and said, "Come again, is this supposed to be some sick joke, or are you and your brother currently on drugs?"

Tommy replied, "I understand that all of this is hard to comprehend right now, but it's the truth. Toby and I are just glad Uriel found you before the demon did."

Micah came out and asked Michael if he had heard anything from Gabriel regarding his mom and stepdad. He stated he had not, but he was still searching. What Micah didn't know was while the demon was killing Mrs. Pitts, his mom saw Derek leave the house all bloody, which caused her to evacuate her home. Mrs. Wade drove to the base where her husband was working a double shift. He didn't understand what was going on but advised her to stay with him until the morning. She had asked about the boys, questioning whether they were in danger. He attempted to calm her down as he ordered one of the officers to call the county sheriff office and have them send units to the Strokes' residence. He put his arms around his wife and said, "I'm sure our kids are safe. If something happens to them, we will know."

Earlier that morning, the military police notified Mr. Wade that the sheriff's office confirmed the two murders at the location he gave the night before. They also stated there was another murder at 8462, which he knew was Tommy's address. He told his wife that they were leaving as he grabbed his revolver and shotgun from his office. She asked her husband about where they were going. He replied, "We will check the university, the neighborhood, I-Hop, but first, let's stop by Micah's apartment."

Mr. Wade drove like a maniac to his son's apartment. As he was driving, a bright light appeared from the backseat of his car, causing him to drive off the road. They both turned their heads as they witnessed a glowing shaped being in their vehicle. He said, "Do not be frightened, for I am an angel. I have been searching for the two of you. There are a few things that I need to address, but first, can you slow down before you cause an accident."

Mrs. Wade replied, "Start talking but first tell me if my boys are alright."

The archangel stated, "Yes, they are fine, and both are currently at the apartment."

She touched her husband's arm and asked him to reduce his speed. He replied, "Fine, but our boys need to be prepared to explain themselves once we arrive."

Meanwhile, Adrian was attempting to track down any of the cryptids. Charlie asked Isabelle if she genuinely cared for the other cryptids. She told him that she did, but deep down, she just wanted to die. She was tired of feeling trapped and controlled by the demons. She informed him that she had a wonderful life with her husband, but that was centuries ago. He asked her what would happen if Ashmead found out that she was helping us. She responded, "He would probably kill me."

Adrian chimed in and said, "If the demons don't kill you, I promise you I will. Now, will you please shut up and stay focused on the mission at hand?"

She shook her head, saying, "Are Lobos always this much fun to be around?"

Charlie told both of them to shut their mouth as they all continued to search for any possible strays.

Back at the apartment, Gabriel walked in with Mr. and Mrs. Wade. She immediately grabbed her son Micah and threw her arms around him. Before she could ask about her youngest son, Mr. Wade asked what the hell was going on. Michael told them to have a seat so he could begin explaining their current situation. He informed them about how their sons were chosen to be protectors of the human race and that the archangels with supernatural powers appointed them.

Mr. Wade looked at the angel, saying, "Do you expect me to believe this crap."

Before he could say another word, Micah told his stepdad that everything he was saying is true. "Right now, our priority is to get both of you, Mr. Pitts, and Toby to a safe location."

He asked his stepdad if he could house all of them somewhere on the base.

Michael interrupted Micah and said, "No, Gabriel will take you all to a secure location. The four of you are safer with an archangel than you are on a military base." He first teleported the Wades then came back for Toby and her dad. As he went to teleport, Toby purposely let go of her dad's hand as she was left behind with the others.

Tommy said, "Why did you do that? Jason can still find you."

She replied, "I feel safer with you and Micah than I do with an angel. If he wants me, then let's use that to our advantage."

Micah glared at her, saying, "Hell no, we are not using you as bait." Tommy seconded the motion as he told her that she would be staying with Uriel at all times until they find Derek.

# Chapter 7

The Lobos received word that a demon other than Ashmead was using the cryptids for his personal use. Delisle asked the pack where they were getting their information from. One of his trusted advisors told him that he was forced to kill one right outside their camp. He stated that right before he killed him, the creature warned the Lobo of the wrath of Jason and begged him to end his life. The cryptid said, "I would rather die warning someone of his terror than being killed by him. The demon is rounding us up, and if we refuse to hunt the Lobos, then he will kill you."

The alpha looked at his advisor and said, "Let's get prepared just in case the demon comes to our camp."

A few hours away from the Lobo camp, Isabelle, Charlie, and Adrian were still searching for any possible cryptids. She spotted four of them just beyond the trees a couple of yards ahead of them. She asked Adrian to fall back so she could have an opportunity to speak to them. She told him, "If they see you, they will automatically go into attack mode."

Before she could even get a word out, they charged toward her, calling her a traitor. When Charlie witnessed this, he quickly got Isabelle to safety while Adrian attacked, ripping their heads off in the process. As he attacked the last one, the cryptid informed him that he might be able to kill the four of them, but he would not be able to save his father.

Adrian looked at both Charlie and Isabelle saying, "I need one of you to teleport us to my dad immediately; he is in great danger!" They both looked at Adrian and informed him they could not teleport to a location they had never been to. He cursed under his breath as he told them that he would find a way. As he began to run through the forest, the other two had no other choice but to chase after him.

Meanwhile, Jason and his army of cryptids decided to invade the Blue Ridge Mountains. When the lookout saw them approaching, he sent a message to Delisle informing him that they were under attack. The cryptids made easy work of their first line of defense. The alpha ordered a few of his trusted advisors to flee the area and find his son. He also told them to get as many young Lobos to safety as possible. He felt that they might lose this battle fighting, and if he was correct, then he didn't want everyone to die in the process. He ordered his advisors to never look back, no matter the outcome.

While the advisors were getting several dozen Lobos to safety, Adrian was busy finding his way to his father. He got to the end of the passage and saw there was a road. He then decided to wait patiently for someone to drive by. Ten minutes later, a semi-truck came flying down the road, so Adrian pushed Isabelle out into the road causing the driver to slam on his brakes. The driver got out to check on the young lady, but before he could, Adrian tackled him to the ground, saying, "I don't want to hurt you, but I need your truck, disconnect your trailer right now." Adrian told the other two to get in as he started the engine and ripped out the GPS tracking device under the dashboard.

Charlie said, "What the hell is your problem? You never harm a human, and you could have killed Isabelle."

He replied, "You would have done the same thing if you knew a demon was heading directly toward your family. So sit back, relax, and buckle up! We have to make it to camp before they do."

As Jason and the cryptids were getting closer, he instructed them to kill every Lobo they encounter. He decided to leave half of the cryptids back in the woods, while he took a fourth of them with him. He ordered the rest to find the location of the Aces and told them, "Do not return until you do. First, we conquer the Lobos, then we eliminate the Aces, and finally, we take down Ashmead once and for all."

The cryptids were not sure if Jason was insane or if he felt that he really could pull off the impossible. One thing they knew for sure was if they wanted to continue to exist, they better not ever cross this lunatic.

Approaching the entrance to the Lobos camp, Jason instructed all the cryptids to spread out and start attacking. He said, "If I witness just one Lobo escape, then I will begin killing each of you."

One on one, the Lobos had the advantage even though they were hugely outnumbered five to one. Delisle grabbed both his warrior swords, which were extremely sharp and measured two feet long. The alpha took a few blows from the cryptids but managed to kill several dozens in the process. The rest of his people put up a good fight, but they were severely defeated. Instead of retreating, Delisle chose to continue fighting even though he witnessed the bloodshed of so many of his people. Jason made his way through the camp as he ripped off the heads of every Lobo he encountered. When he finally got to Delisle, he asked him if he had any final words. The alpha told him to go to hell.

The demon replied, "You first." And he stabbed him with his sword, leaving his body lying on the ground with the alpha holding his own head.

After driving for about two hours, Adrian finally stopped and said, "Okay, this is the closest we will be able to drive. We will have to walk the rest of the way." Once they arrived, they saw all the bloodshed. It was an absolute massacre; Adrian knew his father and the others never stood a chance. When he did approach his father's body, he fell to the ground screaming in agony. He stood over his body, crying to the point where his eyes became swollen, and his entire body went stiff.

Charlie put his hand on his shoulder as he tried to comfort him. He said, "Even if we got here in time, I don't know what we could have done."

Adrian looked up at him, saying, "I would have died fighting while you teleported as many of my people to safety. That is what we could have done, but now it doesn't matter, I failed my father."

As the guys kept bickering, Isabelle told them to shut up. She told Charlie in a whisper that she could sense a demon approaching. She asked him to leave immediately and take Adrian with him. He picked up his father's body as Charlie teleported both of them back to the truck.

A few seconds later, Ashmead appeared and looked to be extremely confused. He asked Isabelle what had happened and where she had been. She told him that Jason had possessed a human and had declared war on the Lobos and the Aces. His first goal was to attack the Lobos, so she came here to try to stop him.

He looked at her, saying, "So he is challenging me for command. What a stupid fool and the same for you as well. If Jason would have seen you, then you would be dead too. Let's go find the remaining cryptids so that you can lead them away. Jason will not use my creations for his own personal agenda." As they were leaving, Ashmead grabbed Isabelle's hand and said, "I can't lose you. If I do, I might go mad." He leaned over to kiss her.

Back at the car, Charlie asked Adrian where he planned on putting his father's remains.

He said, "Not here, we are heading back home, so my father and our people can have a proper burial."

He then asked, "What if a demon is still present."

He replied, "Then I guess you will go back to your brother while I fight and die with my people." He asked Charlie once more, "Are you going to help me or not?"

He told him he would as he put the bloody swords in the car and grabbed Delisle's legs as they carried him back to camp.

Adrian asked Charlie to get all the dead cryptids and stack them in a pile while he gathered all of his people.

Charlie asked Adrian, "What are we going to do with all the dead cryptids?"

He replied, "I am going to burn their bodies. They are not worth a proper burial." He then transformed into a wolf as he dug holes for each of the fallen Lobos. Once he finished, Charlie placed each Lobo in separate burial plots. Afterward, he helped fill in the trenches until everyone was properly buried. Then Adrian transformed back into his human form. Seconds later, Raphael appeared and asked them to return. He told them they thought Jason and more of the cryptids were coming their way. Adrian replied, "We still need to burn the bodies."

The archangel asked if they could give him a minute so he could show his respect and say a few words for Delisle and the other Lobos. He told them, "Once I am done, I will burn the bodies. It is safer this way, besides I can control the flames, the two of you would end up burning up the entire forest within minutes."

Charlie looked at Adrian and said, "Come on, man, Raphael is right; it's time to go." He told Adrian that he knew he wanted revenge for his father's death, but he had a better chance if they worked together.

He looked at Charlie and said, "Okay, boss, I will follow your lead. Get us back to your brother and the other Aces."

He jokingly said, "Don't call me, boss. I'm just a kid."

Adrian replied, "No, you are mature beyond your years; don't let anyone tell you differently. I am proud to call you my friend and you have definitely earned my respect."

The archangel asked if they were any survivors. Adrian told him that the elders, my father's trusted advisors, got all the kids out before the fighting began. "Today will go down as a tragedy, but at least Jason didn't eliminate my entire race."

The angel laid his hands on both of them as he teleported everyone back home.

# Chapter 8

The Aces were patiently waiting for Charlie and Adrian to arrive. Micah felt guilty and thought he should have gone with them. Michael tried to ease his pain by telling him that the outcome would have been the same regardless. He said, "That is easy for you to say when it's not your people under attack."

The angel looked at him and asked, "Why are you always questioning me when I am here to help?"

Micah told the angel his help was not good enough. "If you were truly helping then, our death count wouldn't be so high." Michael was annoyed and informed him that death occurs every day, and it is a part of life.

Before Micah could reply, Mack pulled him aside and said, "We are not here to point fingers, we are here to protect others and stay alive in the process. Fighting with Michael, Isabelle, or any of the other archangels will not solve any of our current problems."

As soon as Micah saw Adrian, he embraced him and gave his condolences. Adrian thanked him for the kind words but told him there was no time for grief. He informed everyone that it was time to bring the fight to them while trying to locate the remaining Lobos. Micah agreed and said, "We know Jason is heading this way. Let's get ready. Even though we are outnumbered, I still like our chances."

Tommy replied, "I like our chances too, but I would feel better if Toby was nowhere near this apartment when Jason and his friends show up. My priority is keeping her safe, so with that said, we will be leaving now."

Micah replied, "It is foolish and stupid if you think you can protect her on your own. I care about your sister also; I don't want anything horrible to happen to her or you." Tommy grabbed Toby by the wrist and told Micah to get out of the way or he would punch him.

Adrian stood between them and told Micah to let them go. "Tommy is right, and it is best if he gets his sister to a safer location." Micah moved out of their way as he watched them walk out the front door.

Tommy walked toward the semi and asked his sister to get in. He took Delisle's warrior swords out and threw them on the ground. Toby said, "I think it would be wise to take them in case we do run into trouble." He acknowledged his sister as he picked one of them up and placed it behind the passenger seat. She asked her brother two questions, "Where are we going, and aren't you worried about Micah and the rest of the guys?"

He replied, "We are going anywhere that will keep you safe. Micah and Mack are my best friends, but they are focused on the greater good right now and not trying to save Derek. I know he is a piece of work, and he has done some questionable things, but he is still my friend."

Toby replied, "He let a demon possess him, and he killed four people, including mom. There is no love lost for him, the demon is pulling the strings, but he permitted Jason to do so. I want to see both of them dead."

Back at the apartment, Mack approached Adrian and informed him that he could use his bathroom to get cleaned up and showered. He told him, "Just grab some of my clothes since we are the same size, but my Yankee shirts are off-limits."

Adrian fell over laughing, "Don't worry, I will use your special shirts to wipe my ass, and then afterward, I will burn the rest."

Mack replied, "Very funny; you must be a Red Sox fan."

He shook his head, "No, my team is the Baltimore Orioles."

Micah asked both of them to shut up, "We need to make sure we are ready for any possible attack. We can always discuss baseball later."

Meanwhile, Mr. Pitts and the Wades were getting restless and kept asking Gabriel when they would be able to go back and see their children. He informed them that it was still not safe as Jason was preparing to attack the Aces. Mr. Wade said, "Just tell me where the attack will take place, and I will have the military there within minutes."

The angel told them that would not be wise as it would cause mass panic and destruction among the population, plus a lot of innocent people would die. "The other archangels are with your children. They are in good hands, I promise."

Mr. Pitts looked at Gabriel saying, "You are full of crap. I blame you and the other archangels for causing heartache and pain to our families."

Mrs. Wade replied, "I might not ever understand any of this, but we need to stay calm and have faith in God and our boys. I won't blame Gabriel or the other archangels, the boys chose to be protectors, and they will find a way to stop the demons."

As Jason and the other cryptids were getting closer to Micah's apartment, he could sense that Toby was no longer there. He instructed some of the cryptids to keep going and find her new location. Michael asked everyone to come outside because he could feel the cryptids were near. Micah told his brother to stay inside the apartment as he, Mack, and Adrian stood with Michael and Raphael prepared to fight. The cryptids came charging in even though they knew they would probably die. Michael and Raphael realized Jason was not with them, so they decided to venture out to see if they could spot him. They ordered Uriel to stay and assist the Aces until they returned.

Adrian saw that Tommy had thrown his father's sword on the ground, so he ran over to retrieve it as Micah used his force field ability to protect himself against the cryptids. He felt if he used himself as bait, it would allow Mack and Adrian to attack and cut off their heads. Mack yelled out, "I will take the ones on the right; you kill the ones on the left." Adrian was mowing them down as if they were vines in the rainforest. Every time he killed one, he would call out one of the names of his fallen brothers.

As Mack was killing them, he saw one of the creatures jump out from a tree. Micah saw the same thing as he intercepted the cryptid. He held on to its neck as the creature pinned him to the ground. Uriel knocked him off Micah as Adrian stabbed the cryptid in the back of the head.

He looked at Micah, saying, "Don't worry; I got your back BROTHER! You and the other Aces are the only families I have left." The cryptids noticed that their army was decreasing in size, and some of them decided to flee, not wanting to die for a pointless cause.

Mack said, "I think they are throwing in the towel, should we go after them."

Uriel replied, "No, it is finished for now. Help me stack all the dead bodies so we can burn them all."

The bystanders in the street were in shock; they couldn't believe what they had witnessed. Uriel looked at Micah, saying, "We might need a new home base, but for now, let's get out of here. Law enforcement is on their way, and they won't understand any of this madness."

Mack replied, "Are we now looked upon as fugitives?"

The archangel stated, "No, but they will not understand or accept what they just witnessed. Let's go back into the apartment and teleport out of here to the university." Uriel told the Aces that he would make the burning of the bodies look like an illusion to everyone in the streets. "Law enforcement will see a huge bonfire and nothing more, but I won't be able to erase the images of what the bystanders saw today."

Across the way, Isabelle stopped dead in her tracks and told Ashmead that she could sense more cryptids had just perished. He instructed her to keep leading the cryptids they had located further south. He told her not to stop until she hit the Georgia state line. She continued to move the cryptids along but, at the same time, was looking for an opening to break away. Isabelle was conflicted regarding the cryptids. A part of her conscience wanted to help them, and the other half wanted to kill all the cryptids, including herself. She just wanted to die and stop being a slave to the demons. She sincerely hoped with the help from Micah and the other Aces, that one day, she could finally put an end to everything. Unfortunately, for now, she had to deal with two insane, psychopath demons. One that was in love with her and the other one that wanted to kill her. No matter what she did, she would never be able to win.

Back at the university, Micah asked Uriel what he and Mack should do about everyone that had witnessed their abilities. He said, "I'm sure we will be on the news. Heck I'm almost positive clips of us fighting are already uploaded on the internet."

Before he could say another word, Michael and Raphael reappeared. They told the Aces that there was no sign of Jason anywhere.

Micah replied, "Of course, he is nowhere in sight, but did you not hear about our current dilemma?"

Michael replied, "Just calm down. Your neighbors witnessed a half-man, half-wolf-like creature attacking and killing bloodsuckers. The other two were individuals standing still having creatures bounce off of them and a man that had swords for arms. Do you truly believe anyone will believe your neighbors? They will attempt to say that mutants were fighting vampires; then, a week later, everyone will forget the whole ordeal."

Micah looked at the angel, saying, "I hope you are right. If not, then we have just painted a huge target on our backs."

A few hours later, Toby tried to once again reason with Tommy asking him to please head back. She said, "Aren't you worried about your friends? Do you think that everyone survived the attack, and most importantly, do you think the angels were able to stop Jason?"

He replied, "If they have stopped Jason, that means Derek is dead. Why does it seem like I am the only one trying to save his life? Should he pay for his crimes and his stupidity? Yes, of course, but not with his life."

She grabbed her brother's hand, saying, "You are right, and I'm with you. Let's try to stop Jason's reign of terror and also save Derek's life."

Tommy was about to squeeze Toby's hand when he looked up and saw dozens of cryptids marching directly toward them. He stopped the almost immediately and reached behind Toby's seat for the sword. He told his sister to leave and drive straight back to Micah. If he and the angels are not there, then just keep on driving. She grabbed her brother's arm, pleading with him not to get out of the truck. He said, "I have to keep you safe even if that means I might die. Now go." And he hugged her goodbye.

# Chapter 9

Toby looked at her brother as she slid over into the driver's seat. She witnessed dozens of cryptids approximately forty yards out in front of them. Instead of turning around as her brother asked, Toby decided to drive straight toward them, hoping to kill as many as possible. As she continued driving down the road, she could see Tommy killing the remaining cryptids. She felt better that she helped him kill some of them and knew he would eventually find his way back to her. Toby was hoping that the Aces survived the attack, especially Micah. She knew she always had feelings for him and was happy that he felt the same about her. It was hard worrying about both Micah and Tommy because losing either one would be devastating for her. Furthermore, she didn't want either one of them to die trying to protect her.

Back at the hotel, the Wades and Mr. Pitts were getting restless and told Gabriel they were leaving. The archangel asked them if they even knew their current location.

Mr. Wade said, "We are somewhere in New York, that I do know. Why do you consider this place safe, we are in a high populated area?"

Gabriel replied, "Most cryptids don't cross into the major cities, and demons don't like to attack in populated places where their existence might be exposed. So we have used this particular hotel room as a safe and secure location for the last fifty years."

Mr. Pitts stood up and said, "Well, it's time for us to check out, it's past the 11th hour." He then threatened to punch someone or something if he had to stay another minute. As he headed toward the door, the archangel pleaded with him to sit back down, but he refused while saying, "You can't keep me here as a prisoner, now move out of my way."

As soon as he opened the door, Jason grabbed him and threw him back. Gabriel reached for his dagger and lunged toward the demon. They fought and rolled around on the floor until he stabbed Jason in the chest. Unfortunately, the demon left Derek's vessel as the dagger hit his lung.

While Mrs. Wade jumped on his chest as she started to perform CPR, Mr. Pitts yelled out, "Let him die!" Several minutes later, Derek was gone.

Gabriel picked up Derek's dead body and asked everyone to lay their hands on him so he could teleport them back home. They asked the angel where they were going, Gabriel told them he was taking them back to the Pitts' residence. He knew it is the last place Jason will check because the demon knew Toby was too scared to return home. The archangel informed Michael what had happened and told him they were back. He asked Gabriel to keep everyone safe until they could get there. He acknowledged the hierarchy as he informed everyone to settle in until the Aces and remaining angels arrived.

Meanwhile, Adrian told Micah he was leaving, but he would return. He told him that he needed to locate the remaining Lobos and make sure they were in a safe place. Adrian gave him a beacon and told him if he needed anything just to press the button, and he would hear the signal and be able to find him. Micah laughed, "So this beacon is like a dog whistle. I am impressed!"

He just stared back at him, saying, "Call it a dog whistle again, and I will insert the beacon up your ass."

Charlie replied, "Don't worry, he won't. He likes to joke around after a dramatic event, plus he misses his girlfriend." Micah told his brother to shut up as he shook Adrian's hand and wished him the best of luck.

Michael told the other two angels they were leaving. Charlie asked where they were going now. The archangel replied, "We are going to the Pitts' residence, Gabriel has brought your parents and Mr. Pitts back after Jason visited them."

Micah asked, "Is Jason dead, and what about Derek?"

He told the Aces that Gabriel stabbed the demon because he had attacked him. Unfortunately, as soon as the dagger hit the skin, the demon abandoned his vessel, leaving Derek to bleed to death.

With mixed emotions, Micah just looked at everyone and said, "How do we begin to explain this to Tommy, they were like brothers?"

Michael replied, "It was either the angel killed the demon, or he would have killed your family. Right now, Jason cannot hurt anyone until he finds a new vessel which knowing him won't take too long. The only demon that can attack in his natural form is Ashmead." Even though there was another that the archangels failed to mention. A few seconds later, they were all reunited back with Gabriel.

As soon as everyone arrived, Mr. Pitts immediately asked about Tommy and Toby. Micah informed him that right before the attack; Tommy took it upon himself to take his sister somewhere safe.

He said, "Somewhere safe, my ass, we were in a secure location and that bastard still found us. There is no such thing as a safe location. Our next mission should be to burn his body and find my children." Micah tried to keep Mr. Pitts calm as he told him that finding them was everyone's top priority. Michael asked Uriel to go search for them. No one knew that they had split up and were in two different locations.

Uriel started following Tommy's trail when he noticed that something or someone caused them to stop and split up. He sensed the direction Toby had gone, so he kept following the other trail. The archangel felt that Toby was probably trying to find her way back as instructed by her brother. He was right as he finally tracked down Tommy a few miles down the road. He told Uriel that they were under attack by a few dozen cryptids, and he dragged all of the dead creatures into the woods. Tommy didn't want to leave the bodies on the road and knew if he had burned them; it would have drawn some unwanted attention. The angel told him that he made the right choice, but right now, they needed to go and re-group with the others.

Tommy said, "You are right; now let's go and find my sister."

A few miles away from where Uriel found Tommy, Jason was out looking for a new vessel. He wanted to inhabit Toby or Tommy's father, but he knew no matter what he did, they would never give consent. The two of them would both choose death before making a deal with a demon. The demon eventually came across a bar and saw an opportunity to pick his next victim. He thought to himself, intoxicated individuals are always the easiest to convince, and laughed out loud. He floated into the bar and saw a gentleman sitting in the corner, drinking his worries away.

Jason whispered in his ear, "Why are you so sad?"

The biker looking around said, "My wife cheated on me and left me for my best friend, my life is officially over."

The demon whispered again, "I can make all your problems go away if you let me in and together we will make them pay. Do you want my help, if so you only have to say the magic word 'YES'?"

The individual replied, "Yes, of course, I want my friend to die and my wife to pay for her sins."

As soon as he heard the word "yes," Jason was in and ready to move forward.

Jason told the drunk that it was time to go. The drunk, not knowing what had just occurred, asked, "I feel trapped, and I have no control of my movement or actions. What did you do to me?"

The demon replied, "Nothing, you permitted me to possess you, now let's go and kill your friend and wife. A promise is a promise, and I always keep my end of the bargain."

Jason asked the vessel what his name was, and he replied, "Go to hell, you bastard."

The demon just laughed, saying, "Okay, since you have such a long name, I will call you Dick for short." Jason told

Dick to keep his mouth shut as he got onto his bike and rode off to find his friend and cheating, unfaithful wife.

Meanwhile, Isabelle knew she had to make a decision soon before Jason found her and the other cryptids. She thought it would be best to see Adrian and inform him of the new location of the cryptids. The cryptids would never be free, and they would always be used as servants to the demons. This is something that Isabelle wanted to put a stop to permanently. She felt the only way cryptids would ever be free is if they were all dead. So she left them in the woods alongside Interstate 95 and ordered them to stay put until further notice. Once they were settled, Isabelle was off to find Adrian, hoping he would listen to her and assist.

She left the cryptids and didn't look back as she went on her way back to Virginia. She was hoping that Adrian was still with Micah and Charlie. The hard part would be to convince Adrian to come with her while keeping it from the Aces. Micah would tell her that it was a suicide mission for him to go alone, plus he still didn't trust her. She knew he would think Adrian was way too emotional right now to wage war on the cryptids. He would be going in with tunnel vision, which would be extremely dangerous and could get him killed. Either way, Isabelle didn't care and just wanted the torment to end for her and her people.

As Tommy and Uriel arrived at his parent's house, Mr. Pitts embraced his son, asking him the whereabouts of his sister. He informed his dad that they were forced to split up after they encountered some cryptids along the way. Tommy promised his dad that they would see her again very soon. He looked at his son, saying, "Don't make any promises that you can't keep. You should have never left her sight."

Tommy replied, "We had to split up, I couldn't keep her safe and fight off the creatures at the same time. There were too many of them, and I would have lost if I didn't have Adrian's warrior sword with me."

Micah intervened, "We will find her, but first I need to tell you something."

Tommy followed Micah into the next room, where he saw Derek's body lying on the dining room table. As soon as he spotted his friend, Tommy dropped to his knees with tears in his eyes. He asked Micah who had killed Derek and how long he had been dead. Micah said, "The demon possessing him tried to attack your dad and my parents. Gabriel tried to stop him without hurting him. He ended up stabbing him in the chest, hoping to kill Jason, but unfortunately, he left Derek's body as the dagger entered the rib cage."

He told Tommy that his mother attempted to save him, but she was unable to as he bled out too fast. Tommy stood up and stared at Gabriel saying, "I hope you are happy. I hope all of you are happy. I thought angels couldn't hurt or kill a human being, but yet here lies my friend on my father's dining room table."

The archangel told him, "The moment Jason possessed Derek's body was the moment your friend died. There was only one way things were going to end for your friend, and death was the only option."

Tommy looked up at Micah and asked if he and the other Aces would help him carry Derek's body to the backyard. Micah and Charlie each grabbed one of his legs as Mack picked him up by the arms. As they walked toward the back, Tommy unlocked and opened the door for them. He looked at the Aces and asked if they would start searching for Toby while he buried and paid his respects to his friend. Micah put his arm around Tommy and told him how very sorry he was that they couldn't save him. He said, "We are leaving now, and I won't come back until we locate your sister."

The three Aces left immediately and went out searching, each heading in a different direction.

# Chapter 10

While riding down the road, Jason asked Dick the name of his friend, and could he so kindly tell him his home address.

Dick replied, "You are not getting near my wife."

The demon replied, "That is an incorrect answer," as he broke one of his fingers. "We can do this all day; you do realize you have nine more digits I can break. Plus two arms, two legs, one neck, and multiple ribs." Jason laughed. "Don't worry; you don't have to tell me. I will just check your cell phone and retrieve the information."

Jason dialed the first number that was listed on his phone, assuming it was his wife. The demon was correct as a female answered the phone. He told her that he would be working late and that she should go out and enjoy herself tonight, and he would see her tomorrow. The woman was shocked to hear from her husband as she told him that she would take his advice and invite a friend over. His wife then said, "I will see you tomorrow Doug, don't work too hard."

As the demon ended the call, he said, "Your name is Doug. No wonder your wife doesn't want you. I bet she refers to you as Dick as well."

Jason decided to stop at a local steakhouse to burn some time and throw back a couple of beers. He went in and sat at the bar as he told Dick flirting with the waitresses was out of the question. The demon said, "I don't have a chance in hell while I'm in this meat suit of yours. You are one sweaty, smelly, hairy, ugly, and overweight joke of a man. This is just another reason why your wife doesn't want your ass." He sat back and ordered a few appetizers, a rib-eye steak, a stack of ribs, a basket of fries, and a couple of drinks. "It is a good thing you are a fat man, or I would never be able to enjoy all of this delicious food."

The demon could sense that Dick was boiling mad inside, and he was enjoying every minute of it. Jason told him, "Don't worry, because as soon as it gets dark, we will leave and say hello to the wife, and if she gives us any lip, we will silence her."

As the sun was setting, Jason threw back his last drink and paid the waitress. He told Dick that it was time to say goodbye to the missus as he rode off on his motorcycle. Once he arrived at Dick's house, he saw two cars in the driveway. Jason said, "Looks like someone is enjoying your wife; let's go inside and say hello." The demon walked up the staircase and saw the spouse and his friend naked in bed.

The wife screamed and said, "Doug, what are you doing here? You told me you weren't coming home until tomorrow."

Doug, being completely devastated, told Jason to go ahead, "You are right, they deserve to die."

Jason ripped out their tongues and broke off both of their legs. He said, "My work here is done; they no longer can scream for help and won't be running to cach other having sex anymore. If they are lucky, someone will eventually find them. Okay, Dick. Let's go, I have a girl to find."

Meanwhile, Ashmead had finally located and gathered all the remaining cryptids. He led them to the exact spot he instructed Isabelle to wait for him. When Ashmead finally arrived and saw that she was gone, he was beyond furious. He told the cryptids that from now on, they have permission to feed and attack any human they desire. Before he left the cryptids, Ashmead also told them going forward; they can only take orders from him directly. If he finds out any of his creatures end up defying him, then the penalty would be death. As the cryptids began to scatter, Ashmead stood there in silence, wondering where Isabelle had gone and how come she deliberately disobeyed him. He thought to himself if this had been any other person, he would just kill them. However, Isabelle wasn't just anyone, which meant he had no idea what he planned to do once he found her.

Mack went back to the area where the archangel found Tommy hoping Toby had doubled back to look for her brother. Charlie checked out the list that Tommy had given him. It was a list of her favorite places and the address to a few of her close friends. Micah, on the other hand, thought Toby would be searching for him. He drove to the university than to the community college she was attending, and then he doubled back to check at his apartment. Micah even thought maybe she would drive to the ice cream parlor or the theater. It would be smart for her to be in a populated area. He was about to head back when he saw the semi at the end of the street.

Micah got out of his car and started to check out the local shops and restaurants to see if he could locate her. As he came out of one of the stores, he saw a biker drop his keys. He picked them up and said, "Be careful with your keys, someone might hijack that nice motorcycle of yours."

The demon replied, "Thank you, kind sir, my buddy Dick would be pissed at me if anything ever happened to his precious bike. You are a gentleman and a scholar. Maybe we will run into each other again one day." Micah thought the biker was very odd as he handed him the keys. He told him to be safe and to have a nice day. As Jason walked away, he thought to himself, *Don't worry, my precious little Ace. Every single day is fantastic, and we will, for sure, be seeing each other again very soon.*

Toby was sitting in the café at the end of the street. As she was finishing her coffee, she thought to herself where on earth could Micah and the other Aces possibly be. She paid for her meal and got up to leave. Toby walked out of the café and saw a fat biker heading her way. As she approached him, he said, "Good afternoon, ma'am, you are incredibly beautiful may I buy you a drink."

She replied, "Thank you for the kind offer, but I have a boyfriend. I am here to meet him."

The demon told her that her boyfriend saw her sitting in the café and walked away. She laughed, saying, "You don't even know who my boyfriend is. Now, if you will excuse me, I have to go."

He stared at her with his red eyes, saying, "I don't think you will be going anywhere. I apologize for meeting you in this disgusting vessel, but an angel destroyed the last one I had."

Toby then realized who he was and decided to turn around and haul ass. She started to scream as she was completely terrified.

Two blocks over as Micah was preparing to drive away, he heard Toby screaming bloody murder. He began running in the direction of her screams. As he ran down the street, he called Charlie and told him to get Tommy and meet him down by the café their mom always went to every morning, "Let him know I located Toby, and I think she is in danger."

Charlie teleported back to the house to retrieve Tommy as Micah tried to reach his girlfriend. Once he made it to the back alley, he saw the fat biker standing over her. Completely shocked that the individual was, in fact, a demon, he tried to trap him within a force field. Micah looked at the biker, who appeared to be unconscious and said, "I have you now, you demon bastard. You won't be hurting her today."

Jason reappeared and shouted, "Nice try," as he lunged toward Toby cutting and stabbing her repeatedly. When Micah saw this, he shifted the force field on Toby as the vessel collapsed to the ground. Micah ran over to Toby holding her butchered body as Jason disappeared into the sky. He told her to stay with him, and help was on the way.

A few seconds later, Isabelle appeared and told Micah that Toby had too many injuries and most likely would die. He looked at her, saying, "NO, she is not going to die! I will not lose her. I can't, I love her." Isabelle told him that she could save her, but he would not like the outcome.

Before he could even reply, Charlie and Tommy came running toward them. Tommy yelled, "Get away from her, you bitch! Micah let's kill her; she is outnumbered three to one."

Micah told Tommy that Jason, not Isabelle, attacked his sister. He bent down next to his sister as Micah held her and said, "I'm so sorry, I promised to keep safe, and I have failed you. Please stay with us, Charlie will get you to a hospital."

Once again, Isabelle told them that she would die before any doctor was able to treat her. Tommy yelled at her again, saying, "What the hell do you suggest we do for Toby!"

Isabelle said, "You have two options. You can watch your sister die in your best friend's arms, or I can save her by turning her."

He replied, "Turn into what, a monster like you? No way. Charlie come, we need to move, and we need to move fast."

Micah grabbed Tommy's arm and said, "Man I don't want her turned either, but she is right. Toby won't survive, she has lost too much blood. This is our only available option if we don't want her to die."

Tommy looked at Micah and said, "I hate you, I promise I will find Jason and you." He stared directly at Isabelle.

Micah nodded at Isabelle as she bit Toby's neck. A few seconds later, the wounds were healed, and her eyes reopened. She looked around at everyone with her now bright yellow eyes as she ripped herself from Micah's arms. Isabelle grabbed her as she fought to set herself free.

Tommy asked, "What's wrong with her? why is she trying to attack us?"

Isabelle replied, "She is a newborn, and she has a desire to hunt. It will take her some time to make sense of everything and remember who you are, along with the other Aces. I need to take her so I can train her to hunt and control her urges to attack humans. Only then will she be safe to be around others."

Tommy said, "I am not going to allow you just to take my sister away."

Charlie replied, "I will take the two of you back then I will stay with Toby and Isabelle. I'm the only one that can keep up with them."

Micah looked at Tommy and said, "We need to go before we get an audience, which won't be good for anyone." Isabelle told Charlie she would wait for him to return as he teleported them back home.

# Chapter 11

Once they arrived back home, Tommy was hot and very angry with Micah. He blamed him for what had happened to his sister and informed everyone that he will kill Jason if it is the last thing he ever does. Micah tried to ensure Tommy that Toby was safe with Isabelle, but hearing those words just infuriated Tommy to the point where he turned around and punched Micah in the face. The archangels ran over to separate the two gentlemen before the altercation escalated any further.

Michael looked at Micah, saying, "So Jason tried to kill Toby, then Isabelle turned her, and now a wild newborn is with her and your brother. Oh, this is not good at all! Cryptids are bad news, but a newborn is a hundred times more dangerous and extremely unpredictable. What makes matters worse is Jason can use her as a weapon if he learns that she is now a cryptid. Which puts your brother in further danger!"

Mr. Pitts and Mr. Wade walked up to Micah and asked if this was true. He replied, "Yes, I tried to save her, but I failed. If Toby weren't turned, then she would have died. Maybe I was selfish, but I couldn't live with myself if she had died."

Micah lowered his head as he began to cry. He apologized to everyone in the room and told them that he was very sorry that he couldn't save her. Mrs. Wade put her arms around her son and said, "You did all you could to save her. If it weren't for your abilities, then she would have died, and you probably would have as well. So please stop feeling sorry for yourself and get up and go after this demon before he finds his next vessel."

Tommy replied, "Your mom is right, let's go." He offered his hand to Micah.

Meanwhile, about forty miles away, Isabelle was wrestling with Toby as she was trying to train her. She first taught her to control her urges to kill humans and focus on hunting deer, cows, and other livestock. Toby was halfway listening as she was attempting to kill squirrels and rabbits. She would even occasionally charge toward Charlie, but fortunately, he was always able to teleport away from her. Isabelle stood next to Charlie and held his arm to her mouth and said, "Biting humans is bad because they are our friend."

He replied, "It seems like Toby is truly struggling with her urge to attack me while you have mastered your desire to harm humans."

Isabelle laughed, saying, "No sweetheart, you have it all wrong. I truly do want to attack you but have learned to restrain myself because I don't want to become a monster. Toby is the first human I have ever bitten in my two hundred plus years as a cryptid. The first twenty-four hours are the hardest; after that, she should start to calm down. Let's take turns watching her so we both can try and get some rest."

Charlie replied, "Sounds good to me."

Back at the Pitt's residence, Ashmead appeared in front of the Aces and archangels. Before he could even say a word, all four angels drew their daggers. The demon said, "I know you hate me, and I hate you. I get it; this is the last place I want to be. I am not here to fight or hurt any of you. We have a common enemy, and if he is not stopped, then the carnage and death toll will just continue to increase."

Michael replied, "Angels do not help or assist demons. We will stop Jason, and then we will come for you."

Ashmead called Michael a fool and told him that this would be the only time he would offer to help them. He informed them that Jason would take upon as many vessels as he sees fit and will never stop killing innocent humans. He looked at Tommy, saying, "He killed your friend, your mother, and your sister just for fun. What do you think he has planned for an encore? Have it your way, but deep down, you know I'm right." And he vanished from the room.

Tommy looked at Michael and said, "He doesn't know Toby is still alive. Is that good or bad news?"

Michael replied, "Good news. If he knew what his precious Isabelle did, he would most likely kill both of them. He is the demon who created cryptids, and Isabelle is his favorite."

Mack commented, "For being one of the top demons, he doesn't seem to be very threatening."

Raphael replied, "Ashmead is very dangerous; he is Lucifer's first in command. He must feel threatened by Jason because this is the first time in years that he has made himself visual to us. Ashmead is horrible, but if Jason takes over hell, then things will most definitely get a hundred times worse."

Michael informed everyone that it was time to take the fight to Jason. He instructed Gabriel to stay behind and protect the parents while they locate and destroy this demon for good. Micah told Gabriel, "If Charlie returns then asks him to remain here with you. He will be able to help you, plus it would keep him safe."

Gabriel replied, "I can't make any guarantees. You do realize he has a mind of his own just like you, and nothing stops him from doing what he wants."

"Yes, that is true, but he listens and trusts you as much as he does me. The only thing I'm saying is to try; he can only teleport to us if he knows our location."

Micah, Tommy, Mack, and the archangels were off to locate Jason. Tommy recommended they start where they last saw him. Michael said, "Micah will head right with me, Raphael go left with Mack, and Tommy and Uriel keep following the trail straight ahead. If you locate him call out to us, and we will be there within seconds."

Micah and Tommy had other ideas, and calling for help was not one of them. They both wanted to witness Jason's death, but Micah wondered how they could kill him without having support from the archangels.

Meanwhile, Jason was searching for his next victim. As he was walking, he saw a young lady stranded on the side of the road. He thought to himself how much fun it would be to possess a woman and how the Aces would never expect it. As the young lady was looking at the busted hose under the hood, he whispered, "I can help fix your car."

She looked down the road and saw that there was no one around her. The young lady, feeling confused and very tired, said to herself, "Why me? This stupid ass car breaks down more than it runs."

Again, the demon said, "Just say yes, and I will enter your hood and make you feel better."

At this point, the woman getting extremely irritated, said, "Yes, imaginary person, please look under my hood and fix my car. I don't care; just get this piece of shit running." Before she could finish complaining, he took her as his new vessel.

Jason melted the hose back on and told the lady they were going to search for a new vehicle. He said, "You are a beautiful girl. What's your name?"

The woman not understanding what had just occurred replied, "I'm Kayla. Am I being possessed? If so please let me go, I didn't do anything to you."

The demon laughed, saying, "Don't worry, I will kill you slowly once I'm done with you. After I get us a new car, I'm going to introduce you to your new boyfriend. So make sure you flirt a lot and let down your hair." Jason could hear her screaming within as he started the car and drove away.

Uriel and Tommy followed the demon's trail that took them through the woods and eventually out onto a county road. Tommy asked how an archangel could always track a demon, and he replied, "Because they smell like burnt roadkill. It is a smell you never forget." The archangel stopped in his tracks. "I lost the scent. He must have driven away, which means he found his new vessel."

Tommy stomped his foot and cursed multiple times. He was beyond livid. "This sucks! We are back to square one, and to make matters worse, we have no idea what Jason looks like now."

Uriel asked Tommy to calm down because they would eventually locate and kill Jason. He said, "We just need to remain patient. We will eventually get him."

Tommy just shook his head, saying, "Being patient has gotten Derek killed and my sister turned into a monster. I apologize if I'm not as understanding as you are. Let's go and meet up with the others. I'm sure Jason is heading back into the city."

Tommy called Micah and told him that Jason had found a new vessel, and he was probably heading back into town. He informed him that he and Uriel were going back to his dad's house, and they should do the same. Micah replied, "Sounds good. Go ahead and inform Mack of the latest details and we will see you there." Tommy kept trying to contact Mack, but his phone went to voicemail every time. Uriel told him that his friend would be fine, and they would both return as soon as he listened to his messages. The archangel placed his hand on Tommy's shoulder as they both teleported back home.

The reason Tommy couldn't get through to Mack was that he was on the phone with Charlie. Mack answered the phone and first asked if everything was alright. Charlie told him it had been a long process, but they were starting to get through to Toby. Mack told him he was surprised he didn't call his brother instead. He stated he tried to call, but his phone was busy. He asked Mack if they had any luck tracking down Jason. He replied, "No, we have not, but

Ashmead did come to visit us. He feels that Jason is a great threat, and if he is not stopped, then there will be additional chaos and even more deaths. The archangels agreed with Ashmead but told him that angels do not help demons."

Charlie told him that he had to go since it was his turn to watch Toby. He asked Mack to keep him updated and continue to make sure his parents are safe. Mack replied, "Sure thing, buddy," as he said goodbye.

Mack was asking Raphael if they should continue looking for Jason when out of nowhere, a car came flying around the corner. It was Jason within his new vessel, 'Kayla' but Mack didn't know. She crashed into a street light as she drove up onto the sidewalk.

She stumbled out of the car and called out to Mack, "Hey, mister, can you help me? I'm scared and don't know what to do." He walked over to her, asking for her name. She replied, "My name is Kayla, I feel like a ghost, or something was after me. I know you probably think that I am crazy, but can you help me?" Mack told her to take a deep breath and assured her that everything would be just fine. She threw her arms around him while thanking him over and over again.

He said, "Okay, sweetie, you can let go of me. My friend and I will get you back home. Can you give us your address?"

The demon saw that Mack was with Raphael and declined his offer. She told Mack that he was extremely kind, and he had helped her more than enough. She told him that he should go and after she took care of her car, she would walk home. At that very moment, two officers arrived at the scene of the accident. Mack gave her his phone number and told her to call him anytime. She kissed him on the cheek right before she started to inform the officer what had happened.

As he walked toward Raphael, he stated, "Let's keep moving. I can sense Jason is nearby." Neither one of them realized that the young lady was the new vessel.

# Chapter 12

Raphael told Mack that he believed one of the officers could be Jason. He asked the archangel if they should confront him. He said no, that would cause us exposure that they didn't need. He asked Mack to take a photo of each cop, and they would follow up once they regrouped with the others. He took several pictures of the officers but also took some of Kayla. He asked Raphael if he thought she was pretty. He replied, "Yes, she is PRETTY crazy. She drove like a maniac wrapping her car around a light pole. Trust me, don't let her sexy body and cute smile confuse you."

Mack put his arm around him, saying, "Don't be a grumpy archangel, it's not a very good look for you."

Raphael looked at him and said, "I'm going to ignore that last comment you made. Let's go."

Back at the Pitts' residence, Raphael pulled Michael to the side and told him that he believed Jason currently possessed a police officer. He told him that he didn't approach them because it was a populated area with several bystanders around the scene. Michael informed him that he made the right call, but they do need to act quickly because the body count is getting too high. "There are lots of questions coming from everyone within the community. If it continues, it may cause mass panic for the entire city."

Raphael told the hierarchy that Mack took pictures of both gentlemen.

He replied, "Good, I will get with him and then pay a visit to the two officers. I hope you are right, and I can finally stop Jason's reign of terror."

Michael went to find the two officers; he finally caught up with them at a Shell gas station. He acted as a customer by buying a soda and a bag of chips. He looked over at the officers and said, "Gentlemen, which scratch-off should I purchase. If you pick one, maybe I will win."

One of them replied, "The green one since the color represents luck."

He replied, "Thanks, I appreciate it." As he walked out of the store, he told the cashier to keep the change. She looked up to say thank you, but Michael was already gone.

As Michael was walking back to the scene of the accident, he gave the chips and soda to a homeless man. He thought to himself, Jason didn't possess the cops because that would have drawn too much attention. The bystanders were just other drivers and people around the area, so that just left the girl. Michael's eyes lit up. "That's it, the girl that spoke to Mack is Jason's new vessel," he said to himself. "I need to get back and tell the other archangels before Jason realizes we have figured it out." He teleported back, hoping that Mack was still there.

Meanwhile, Ashmead was still searching for both Jason and Isabelle. He was hoping the archangels would find Jason first because he only had the power to trap him, not kill him. Ashmead could only possess humans, create and kill cryptids, and kill the low-level demons. The high ranking demons that were part of Lucifer's army could only be killed by an archangel's dagger or the devil himself. He wanted nothing more than for Jason to be destroyed, Isabelle to fall in love with him, and the Aces to crumble and fall. Once Jason was taken care of, he had an idea that would ultimately destroy the Aces forever. The only thing he wasn't sure of was Isabelle and her loyalty to him and his cause.

Minutes before Michael returned to the others; Mack received a call from Kayla. He answered the call, hearing the fear in her voice. She told him that it wasn't a ghost she was running from, but a demon. She said, "I know you probably think I'm crazy, but I'm not. I am scared that this demon spawn is going to kill me once it gets ahold of me."

He replied, "Don't move, and please give me your address. I will be there in a few minutes." She texted him her address as he was walking to his car. He told her once more, "Stay right there, I will get you and take you somewhere safe."

Michael arrived back at Mr. Pitts' house and immediately asked if Mack was still here. Raphael informed him that he had just left two minutes ago. Michael said, "We need to track his phone and find out where he is going before it's too late." Micah asked what was going on. The archangel replied, "The girl Mack met earlier today is Jason. And if we don't find him first, the demon will kill him."

Mr. Wade told Michael that his friend Victor Richardson could trace his phone. He placed a call to him and gave him Mack's number. As soon as they were given his location, the angels and Aces teleported directly to that address. Once they arrived, they found Mack in one of the bedrooms. He was badly injured and bleeding but still alive. He looked at Micah and said, "Kayla is Jason, I tried to stop him, but he got away. The good news is I did hurt him."

Micah replied, "Don't worry about that now. We are going to get you to a hospital."

Micah and Tommy assisted their friend to the emergency room. Mack had several cuts and lashes on his chest and legs. The nurse asked what happened, and he stated that the girl he was seeing got mad at him. She asked if Mack wanted to make a report against this woman. He told the nurse no; he just wanted to focus on healing his wounds. She said, "I hope you don't plan on seeing this psycho girl again."

Mack replied, "Nope, I am done with online dating. I will stick to dating college girls that attend my university."

Tommy just looked at him as the nurse left the room, "Really, online dating! Next time, please come up with something better than that garbage."

He replied, "No, next time, I won't lose my mind when a beautiful woman winks at me."

Raphael told the guys to knock it off and find Jason. He promised the Aces that he would stay with Mack until he was ready to be discharged.

As the guys were leaving, Tommy told Micah they needed Charlie and Adrian to return. He said, "We need to end this now. Jason has caused too much pain for all of us, especially me. I mean Mack was fortunate; my mom, sister, and Derek not so much."

Micah replied, "I know, his reign of terror has to end, no matter what."

Tommy informed his friend that when they do find the demon, he would be the one that killed him. "Do not try to talk me out of it either; it is not up for negotiation."

Micah stated that he understood as he took out his cell phone to call his brother.

Charlie saw that his brother was calling as he answered his phone. Micah told him that they needed his help tracking down Jason. He went on to tell him how the demon attacked and wounded Mack. He asked Micah where Mack was currently. Micah replied, "He is in the hospital recovering, and Raphael is with him."

Before Charlie could say another word, Toby took the phone from him. She told Micah that she missed him and her brother dearly. She asked him what she could do to help because she could not sit around any longer. She told Micah to give Charlie their location, and they would both be there in a second. He tried to tell her that it was too dangerous. He was worried if, given the opportunity, he would finish killing her.

Toby replied, "I am coming back with your brother with or without your consent. I want to kiss you when I return, but if you piss me off, I might bite you instead. But don't worry; I am learning to control my urges for human blood." He instructed her to go to her father's house, and they would meet them there.

Tommy and Micah arrived back to the house minutes after Charlie and Toby showed up. Michael asked who had given her permission to return. Before Micah could reply, Mr. Pitts stated that she was his only daughter, and she would always be welcome here in his house. Tommy told the other archangels that she would be okay because she had learned to master her desire for human blood. Micah asked Toby why Isabelle had not come with them. She asked him to kiss her before she answered any of his questions. He walked over to her and kissed her multiple times. He looked at her, saying, "You truly have mastered your desire not to hunt or harm humans."

She replied, "No, I very much wanted to bite your lips off, but Isabelle taught me not to hurt people that would never hurt me." She eventually answered Micah's question and told him that she had to get back to the other cryptids before Ashmead got suspicious.

Michael told everyone they could no longer wait for Jason to strike again. He asked Uriel to stay and watch over Mr. Pitts, Toby, and Charlie's parents. Toby replied, "No, I go where my brother goes. And I won't stop until Jason is dead. He can't hurt me anymore, and I refuse to live in fear."

The archangel replied, "Fine, you can come, but I can't guarantee your safety. My alliance lies with God. My sole purpose is to protect the Aces and all the other humans in the world. In my opinion, you are already dead."

When Tommy heard this, he got in Michael's face, yelling and screaming at him. He told him that he better not act like his sister's life was not significant. If he did, then he promised him he would regret it.

Micah walked up next to Tommy, saying, "Don't worry, if he does it again, then I will simply quit being an Ace right after I punch him in the face."

Toby replied, "Boys calm down, we are all on the same side. Now let's go, we are wasting precious time."

They all left and broke up into two groups. Toby and Micah went with Michael, while Gabriel took Tommy and

Charlie. Tommy asked his sister to go with Micah because he didn't want her anywhere near him when he killed Jason. Michael and the guys went back to Kayla's house, and Gabriel took the other two and started checking out local hospitals and clinics. Once Michael and the others arrived at Kayla's residence, they found the place trashed, and an elderly couple murdered in the living room. Micah looked around and said, "I'm guessing they are Kayla's grandparents, and whichever car they owned, Jason must have stolen it."

Micah called his stepdad and asked him if his buddy Victor could find out what kind of vehicle Mr. Jon Anderson drove. Mr. Wade told his stepson that he would try and get back to him. Toby told the archangel that if Kayla's last name is also Anderson, then maybe they could figure out where she might go next. Demons have been known to hide behind their vessel's identity whenever needed.

Back at the hospital, Mack was still recovering from his injuries but was eager to leave. Raphael kept telling him to rest and take it easy, but Mack wasn't listening to him. He told the archangel that he should be out there with his friends looking for Jason. The angel replied, "They are searching day and night looking for him. You know your friends will stop at nothing to make sure he is destroyed and sent back to the depths of hell."

Mack replied, "No, hell is too good for a piece of shit like him. He needs to be eliminated from existence."

Raphael told him that justice would be served, and the more he dwells on it, the more his heart will be consumed by hate. He said, "If that occurs, then evil still wins even if

Jason is destroyed. I worry about Tommy. Please don't give me a reason to worry about you as well."

Ten minutes later, Micah's cell phone rang, and he noticed it was his stepdad. He told his stepson that Mr. Anderson had a black 2010 Lincoln Town Car registered under his name. He also said to him that he would try to track his car through the street cameras, and if he found anything, then he would let Micah know. Micah asked his stepdad who this Victor guy was and how did he know him. Mr. Wade replied, "If I told you, then I would have to kill you. Just be careful, I will answer that question when the time is right." He thanked his stepdad for the information as he ended the call.

On the other side of town, Charlie was busy teleporting Tommy to every known clinic and hospital in the surrounding area. He kept telling Charlie that Jason had to be seeking medical attention somewhere because his vessel had a few deep cuts on her. He told Tommy to be patient; they would find him eventually.

Tommy replied, "Be patient, I'm beyond being patient, I am now determined and filled with rage. So please save your pep talk for someone who cares because I'm not the one." Gabriel asked the guys to knock it off as he mentioned to them that maybe they should be checking all the veterinarian hospitals as a secondary option. Those places can stitch up wounds too.

Tommy replied, "Gabriel is right, let's backtrack and check all the animal clinics as well. Just remember, once we locate him, I will be the one ending his life."

# Chapter 13

Meanwhile, Isabelle was making her way back to the other cryptids when she noticed Ashmead was waiting for her. She asked him what he was doing. He replied, "I could ask you the same question. What I want to know right now is where have you been, and why did you deliberately disobey me."

Before she could even respond, he told her to choose her next words very carefully. She told him that she was scanning the surrounding areas making sure no Lobos were around. He stated that was a lie as he tossed her into a cage. He told her that he knew she was trying to free herself and also that she had recently bitten another human being. Ashmead demanded that she tell him why, and he wanted to know the identity of this other person.

She replied, "It was no one. I just felt bad because she was a victim of one of Jason's horrible attacks. I gave her a second chance at life because she didn't deserve to die." He ordered some of the cryptids to find this recent newborn and bring her to him. He told Isabelle that she would stay in the cage until he returned.

Ashmead was livid. He couldn't believe that he had to deal with Isabelle when he was busy trying to stop Jason.

He thought to himself if the archangels refused to help him, then maybe he could convince one of the Aces to assist him instead. He started to laugh as he said, "I know precisely which Ace I should approach. I will make him a deal that he can't refuse." He let the cryptids do their thing as he left to find Tommy. He said to himself, "I bet he would be willing to do anything for his precious sister." The only thing he didn't understand was why Isabelle was willing to help the Aces.

Ashmead finally made his way back to the city where Tommy and the others were still searching. He waited for his moment when he could get Tommy all alone so he could talk to him. Charlie told the other two that they should keep moving because the animal hospitals were showing no traces of Jason ever being there. Gabriel told them to go on to the next one while he checked in with Michael and the others. As soon as they arrived at the next clinic, Ashmead appeared to them.

Charlie told Tommy they needed to leave, and they needed to leave now. Before he could teleport them to a different location, the demon placed his hand on Charlie and instructed him to go to sleep. Tommy ran toward Ashmead, saying, "What did you do to him and give me one good reason why I shouldn't kill you?"

The demon just laughed as he told him, "Charlie is just fine. He will wake up from his nap, feeling like a new man. Now get your ass over here and walk with me so that I can tell you my master plan."

Ashmead told Tommy that only an archangel dagger could kill a demon. He looked at the demon and said, "Yes,

I know, please tell me something useful or get out of my face."

The demon stated, "Yes, but you are not truly listening to me. No one ever said it had to be an archangel who killed the demon; you just need their dagger. Do you get it now, or are you just another stupid human?"

Tommy replied, "No, I hear you loud and clear. Now I know what I need to do to kill Jason."

As Ashmead started to fade away, he said, "Kill Jason for me and I won't murder your sister."

Tommy ran over to Charlie to help him up. When he awoke, he screamed, "Where is Ashmead, and are we dead?"

He replied, "No, we are very much alive, but now I know what I must do to kill Jason and protect everyone else. Come on, get up; we need to keep searching."

Charlie asked what the demon had said to him. He replied, "He told me the secret on how humans can kill demons."

Charlie shook his head, "Wait, what? That makes absolutely no sense; he is a demon; why would he give you instructions on how to kill one." He asked Tommy if they should wait on Gabriel.

He replied, "No, he is an angel he will catch up to us eventually. Now let's go, we are wasting time the longer we stay here."

After waiting several hours, Micah finally said, "I don't think Jason is coming back to this girl's house. He must have found somewhere to lay low. He knows he is being hunted by not only us but Ashmead as well. Hopefully,

Victor will have Jason's location soon, once one of the cameras records his license plate."

Michael told Micah that it was probably best to return home. "We can continue our search once we have additional information."

Toby replied, "Michael is right; we are wasting time by just camping out here at this girl's house. We need to regroup so we will be ready to attack once Victor gives us the new location."

Once they decided to return home, Michael asked Gabriel to retrieve Charlie and Tommy. Micah told everyone while they wait to hear back from Victor, they should take turns visiting Mack in the hospital. Toby thought that was a fantastic idea. She was both sad and furious about what had happened to Mack. She was tired of watching people that she cared about fall victim to Jason's vicious attacks. Even though Toby would certainly rejoice once they did kill Jason, no one would be more thrilled that day than Tommy. Gabriel agreed with everyone as he left to locate both Tommy and Charlie.

The archangel eventually found them at an animal clinic on the edge of town. He told them Michael wanted everyone to return until they got word on Jason's location. Tommy said, "I don't need a location; I will find him myself. We have wasted too much time already by us regrouping. I thought we broke up into teams, and all agreed we wouldn't stop until he was dead."

Gabriel replied, "The trail has gone cold, he could have gone anywhere. Let's wait until we have useful intel before we waste any more time."

Tommy told Gabriel and Charlie that they could do what they want, but he wasn't going back at this time.

At that very moment, Jason appeared and grabbed Charlie. He told Gabriel if he even thinks about reaching for his dagger, he would cut Charlie's throat. The demon looked at Tommy and instructed him, "Return to this exact location at midnight with your sister. I will exchange this precious Ace for the newborn. If not, he dies, and I will still get my hands on Toby eventually. Please don't waste your time trying to calculate a master plan because I always keep my word."

Seconds later, Jason vanished and was nowhere in sight. Tommy looked at Gabriel and said, "Trading my sister is not even an option, so we better come up with a different strategy to save Charlie's life. Let's go, midnight will be here before we know it."

As Tommy returned to his father's house, Micah asked why Charlie wasn't with him. He told Micah that Jason intercepted him and was now trying to use him as a bargaining chip. Tommy stated that if they want him back alive, then they must hand over Toby in return. Micah replied, "We are not negotiating with that piece of shit, but we are getting my brother back."

Michael told the Aces that getting Charlie back was their top priority. "If we have the opportunity to kill Jason in the process, then we will take it."

Both Tommy and Micah stated that it must end tonight. They will save Charlie and find a way to end Jason's reign of terror permanently or die trying.

Michael took Micah to the hospital so he could visit with Mack. He told his friend that Jason had struck again and now had Charlie as his prisoner. Mack said to him that Jason's sole purpose was to kill everything he came in contact with and there was a possibility Charlie was already dead.

He replied, "No, we are not going to think like that. If he wanted my brother dead, then he would have killed him instead of kidnapping him. He says he wants to exchange Charlie for Toby, but I'm not buying it. There is a bigger plan here, and we are probably walking into a trap come midnight." Mack sat up and informed his friend that he was coming with them. He told Micah that he felt eighty percent better, and he wanted to witness Jason's death. Raphael tried to talk him out of it, but Mack wasn't paying him any attention.

Micah replied, "You heard him, Raphael, it's time for all of us to return home."

As Micah, Mack, and Raphael returned, Tommy was outside, clearing his head. He knew he had to kill Jason, but he also wanted to make sure that no one was harmed in the process. As he was pacing back and forth, he heard a whisper asking him if he was getting cold feet. He yelled out to Ashmead that he better leave him alone or kill him. He was over the mind games and knew what had to be done. He also told Ashmead that he would kill him too if he ever mentioned his sister again.

The demon just laughed and said, "I like you, you're funny." And he vanished into the night sky.

Ashmead went back to the camp where he left Isabelle caged up, hoping she would be ready to talk. When he appeared, she asked him to kill her. She told him that she was tired of living as his servant and as a hideous monster.

He replied, "You are my greatest love; you are not a monster. I granted you eternal life when I bit you so many years ago. Why can't you be grateful and love me in return."

She yelled at him, calling him a worthless piece of shit. "You do not love me! You like power and control. Demons are not capable of showing love or compassion. The sole purpose of any demon is to cause chaos and despair for everyone around them. Oh, I almost forgot, you are also nothing more than Lucifer's pet."

When Ashmead heard this, his red eyes filled with rage as he grabbed her through the bars and scratched her face. He said, "You will learn to be obedient, or I will rip the skin from your body until you are dead. Just remember you brought this upon yourself, my love." Seconds later, Ashmead was gone as Isabelle dried the blood from her face.

Once Michael saw that Mack had returned, he automatically started having concerns. He thought unless Mack had fully recovered, he should remain there at the house. Micah told Michael that if his friend stated he was good to go, then he was coming with them. The hierarchy told Micah that all the Aces had a hidden agenda on why Jason needed to die. Michael informed him that he didn't want any of their emotions to cloud their mind tonight. He said, "The Aces' job is to keep Toby safe while he and the other archangels retrieve Charlie and destroy Jason. I hope you plan on following my instructions later. If not, there is a possibility someone may die."

Micah replied, "I give you my word that we will do it your way. I want the same outcome as you do."

# Chapter 14

As the clock ticked closer to midnight, everyone prepared for their epic encounter with Jason. The archangel informed the Aces to be ready for anything. "Jason is the worst demon there is," said Michael, "He may tell us he wants to trade, but in reality, his only desire is to watch people die."

Tommy told Micah to keep a force field around his sister at all times. Toby was offended by her brother and told him that she planned to fight as well. Micah and Tommy both yelled "No!" at the same time. Micah looked at Toby, saying, "For whatever reason, his focus is on you. Which means we must keep you safe. You will not be fighting or engaging in tonight's affair. Please promise me that you will stand back and listen to your brother and me."

She replied, "Fine, I will stay back, but promise me this ends tonight." They both acknowledged Toby as they all headed out.

Once they arrived at the designated location, they noticed Jason was nowhere to be located. As they searched the entire area, they saw a rolling chair with a note pinned to the cushion. The letter read: "I have changed my mind about tonight. Come back the same time tomorrow, but please make sure it is only the three of you. I will let Micah decide which three show up tomorrow as long as one of you is Toby. See you then. Love and kisses, sincerely, your favorite demon."

Tommy threw the chair out the window, saying, "I'm so tired of this bastard. Jason is playing us, and we are letting him. I don't care what you say, Micah, I plan to be one of three coming back tomorrow night." Michael told the Aces that there was nothing more they could do at this moment as they then teleported back home.

Micah told everyone that it would be Tommy, Toby, and Uriel who would return to confront Jason. Michael said, "No, have you lost your mind that is a terrible idea. It will be you, Toby, and I return, and that is final."

Toby replied, "I stand by my boyfriend's decision. If he feels Tommy and Uriel give us our best chance of defeating Jason and rescuing his brother, then I support him. So, Michael, it will be Micah's way or I don't go, and if so, we all lose."

Michael shook his head, saying, "Why is everyone acting so stubborn. How can I help guide everyone if nobody will follow my lead?"

Micah replied, "God gave us the ability to have free will and make our own decisions, so please let me choose. I am the leader. If Toby doesn't go then my brother dies. If I had not chosen Tommy, then he would have never returned with us, and I pick Uriel because frankly, you are pissing me off." Michael being utterly speechless, simply stared at Micah as he walked out the front door.

Jason spent the following day, creating more cryptids and ordered the them to turn as many humans as possible. The Aces had no idea that he held Charlie captive inside a

111

devil's cage at Derek's house. Just like Isabelle, Charlie had nowhere to go. The cages were extremely hot and also took away a person's powers and strength. Jason was preparing to not only eliminate the Aces but the entire human population. He thought Ashmead was weak and didn't have it in him to defeat the Aces. Ashmead believed that there should be chaos but also a sense of balance. Jason felt his mentor had changed and was getting soft since meeting Isabelle. The last thing he was going to tolerate was watching the Lucifer's first-in-command show compassion for others, especially cryptids.

Meanwhile, Ashmead returned to Isabelle, hoping she would reconsider and answer his question. She told him that she had nothing left to say. He told Isabelle that Jason was creating more cryptids, and he needed her help to stop him. He said, "I know you hate me, but I will give you another chance. If you help me destroy Jason and gather all the new cryptids, then I will set you free. If you ever lie to me or recruit the archangels to kill me, then I will end your life. Do we have a deal? This is a one-time offer."

She nodded her head, "Deal, now get me the hell out of this cage." He snapped his fingers, and just like that, he and the cage were gone.

All of a sudden, Isabelle appeared in front of Micah and everyone else. As soon as Tommy saw her, he grabbed and slammed her against the wall. He asked her if she had any final words before he crushed her windpipe. Toby and Micah yelled out to Tommy to stop and kindly asked him to let her go. He unlocked his grip as Isabelle fell to the ground. Toby ran over to her and asked what had happened.

She told them that Ashmead and Jason both know about Toby.

"He locked me in a demon cage and tortured me for helping a human. Ashmead said to me that Jason is currently creating hundreds and hundreds of new cryptids. His goal is to either control or kill all of us, including Toby and me. He won't kill me until the end because he knows that is his only shot at killing Ashmead."

Tommy said, "Right now, we are busy trying to rescue Charlie from Jason, but don't worry. I still plan on killing you later."

Isabelle replied, "You do what you must, but just know he can't contain Charlie and his abilities alone. He must have him trapped in a demon cage like Ashmead had me. If we find the cage, there is a good possibility we find them both."

Isabelle asked if they had checked all previous locations of the individuals Jason had possessed. She stated that demons like to go to places that are familiar and where they feel comfortable. Micah replied, "We need to recheck Kayla's house along with Derek's and the fat man's house." Mack and Raphael were assigned to check the big man's house while Michael and Micah planned to return to Kayla's place.

Tommy said, "I will go next door with Uriel and Toby to double-check Derek's house one last time."

Michael told everyone, "If you locate Charlie, then leave him there until tonight. If we free him beforehand, then Jason will not show up, and we may lose our opportunity to stop him."

Isabelle told them to go while she watched over their parents. Mr. Wade asked everyone to wait a few more minutes until his friend Victor arrived. He told the Aces that he had a gift for them.

Micah asked his stepdad once again about Victor Richardson and how did he know him. Mr. Wade replied, "Mr. Richardson is in charge of surveillance and IT protocols at the base. He is also familiar with both supernatural and spiritual creatures." Before he could say another word, Michael interrupted Mr. Wade and told him Victor Richardson was a former Ace. Mack asked the archangel why Victor was no longer an Ace.

Michael replied, "He was badly injured by a demon, which left him paralyzed from the waist down. I killed the demon that attacked him, but not before he stabbed Victor in the back. He was in the reserves at the time I recruited him, and your stepdad helped him get his current position since his specialty was in cybersecurity and computers."

Micah looked at his stepdad, saying, "Did you also know he was once an Ace?"

Mr. Wade replied, "No, I just thought he was a crazy conspiracy soldier who happened to be good with computers. Michael didn't inform me that he was a former Ace until I first mentioned his name."

Seconds later, there was a knock at the door. Mr. Wade opened the door and invited Victor into the house. He introduced himself to everyone and informed the Aces that he had a gift for each of them. Victor handed each Ace a box which contained a bracelet inside. He told them that the bracelet would detect the vibes of each creature they encounter. He explained if the bracelet turns yellow, then a cryptid is near, and if it turns red, a demon is in the surrounding area. Micah looked down and asked why his bracelet was glowing.

Victor replied, "It glows when you are in the presence of an angel. I wish I had developed these back when I was an Ace. If I had, then maybe I would still be walking." He told the Aces that he was strictly here to help, and no matter how frustrated Michael might make you feel, the archangel is also here to help guide you in the right direction.

Once he met the Aces and said hello to Michael, he asked why there were cryptids present among them. Tommy said, "One of them is my sister and the other one I keep near me so I can kill her if needed. The only reason she is still breathing is that she helped save my sister's life."

Victor replied, "More than one Ace, and now we are teaming up with cryptids, I see a lot of things have changed since I was an Ace."

Isabelle spoke up, saying, "Well, it's good to see you too, Victor. I told you years ago I didn't ask for this life and like always you didn't believe me. I'm sorry Ashmead attacked and paralyzed you; I hate him more than you will ever know."

Michael informed everyone that introductions were officially over, "It is time to break off and search each designated location then report back here immediately."

Once Mack and Raphael arrived at their location, they realized no one ever came looking for the fat man and his wife. Both their bodies were still inside the house, decaying. There was no odor worse than that of a rotting human corpse. The smell was so unbearable that Mack almost vomited in the bedroom where the victim's wife and lover were brutally murdered.

Raphael yelled out to Mack, "There is no cage or signs that Jason has returned since he killed the lovers upstairs. Hopefully, Michael or Uriel will have better luck."

Mack looked at Raphael, saying, "It is probably best that we didn't find him here. If we had, I probably would have done something stupid like getting myself killed. Tommy might hate Jason more, but I will sleep better once he is gone."

The archangel replied, "Stop feeling sorry for yourself. I wish Jason didn't hurt you, but he did. Please remain positive and have confidence in yourself. If not, it will be your undoing that will get you killed not a demon or cryptid. Now let's go before this horrific smell overpowers us."

Michael and Micah teleported back to Kayla's house. They found that there was still police tape in and around the house where the murders had taken place. Micah told Michael that it is unfortunate how Kayla's life will be forever ruined just because she was in the wrong place at the worst possible time. Michael replied, "Yes, it is deplorable, but the bottom line is she did permit him to possess her. I'm sure she was confused and having a terrible day, but ultimately it was her fault. Every decision a person makes good or bad always has a consequence. Out of everything I can and will teach you, that is probably the most important lesson in life."

Micah acknowledged the archangel as he finished searching the house. They both looked at each other, saying, "Wherever Jason went, I don't think he is coming back here. Let's head back; maybe the others had better luck."

Meanwhile, Uriel, Tommy, and Toby returned to Derek's house. Just being there again made Tommy feel pissed off and extremely sad. He still blamed himself every day for his friend's death. Seconds later, Charlie called out from the back bedroom. As they headed that way, the front door opened, and dozens of cryptids started to flood into the house. Toby told Uriel to rescue Charlie, she and her brother would handle the cryptids. She attacked them head-on as she wounded them and tossed them to her brother.

He punched and broke the neck of every cryptid that he got his hands on. Isabelle heard the screams from next door as she ran over to assist them, while Gabriel stayed behind to protect the parents. They eventually fought their way to the back of the house, leaving a pile of dead cryptids in their path. Once they opened the door, they immediately saw Charlie in the cage and Jason standing guard.

The demon said, "I see the Aces suck at following directions. If you want your friend, then I dare you to come and take him from me if you can."

# Chapter 15

As everyone had their eyes glued on Jason, even more cryptids flooded into the house. He laughed, saying, "You can't stop me and save him if you are busy fighting my army. Did you think I wouldn't count your every move? I made things simple for you, hand over Toby, and the kid is yours."

Tommy replied, "Go fuck yourself; you will not be leaving here alive. I will destroy you!"

"Temper, temper, my young inexperienced Ace. I love the hate that you have for me. Didn't Uriel teach you, revenge will eventually be your downfall? You drew the short stick; you see Uriel was the last archangel God created, which means he is the most pathetic one of all."

They fought off as many cryptids as they could, but eventually, they had Isabelle and Toby pinned to the ground. They were instructed earlier to capture them and were told not to harm them under any circumstance. Uriel and Tommy kept fighting and killing as many as they could, but soon they were being pinned against the corner of the room. Uriel told Tommy that they needed to retreat and fight another day with more reinforcements. Tommy replied, "I'm not leaving anyone behind, plus I told you earlier this ends today."

Before he could say another word, he saw Ashmead appear in the cage. Tommy reached for Uriel's dagger as Ashmead grabbed hold of Jason through the bars. Jason yelled, "What are you doing? Let me go; we are on the same side."

The moment he touched the dagger, his hand caught on fire. Screaming in pain, he lunged at Jason, stabbing him multiple times until his vessel collapsed to the ground. When the cryptids witnessed Tommy killing Jason, they all began to flee the area.

Once Tommy saw that Jason was gone, he dropped the dagger and asked Uriel to help him. He touched his arm and extinguished the fire. He told Tommy that his hand was severely burned, and he would most likely lose it. He stared back at Ashmead, saying, "You told me I could kill him with an archangel's dagger. You left out the part where touching it could kill me."

He replied, "He is gone; be grateful his reign of terror is over." Ashmead looked at everyone and told them that next time he encounters them, he wouldn't hesitate to kill any Ace or angel in his presence. He kept his promise and released Isabelle from his control and touched Tommy's hand and turned it to stone. The demon said, "You are healed, the sledgehammer hand looks way cooler than your small monkey fingers." Before Tommy could even reply, Ashmead, the cage, and Kayla's body were gone.

Uriel picked up Charlie as he was suffering from heat exhaustion and dehydration and carried him next door. Once Uriel, Tommy, and the girls returned, Michael asked them what had happened and how come they didn't request any help. Toby replied, "We didn't have time to call for you or anyone else. Jason and about a hundred cryptids were waiting for us once we arrived next door."

Micah walked up and hugged both his brother and friend then kissed Toby. He asked them how they were able to kill Jason and asked about his hand. Tommy replied, "The entire outcome is the result of Ashmead's involvement. He lied to me, and now I am minus one hand. The only upside is we are now free from Jason, and no one else will ever perish because of him."

Michael replied, "Today is definitely a victory for all of us, but just remember every time a demon falls, another one rises."

Several weeks later, things were returning to normal. Tommy and Toby decided to stay and live with their dad. Charlie returned to school but was kicked off the team for being a no-show all week and missing two games. He told the school that he had been deathly sick and got treated at the hospital on base. The school allowed him to make up the work but told him they would not reinstate him on the team. Several scouts lost interest in him; however, some colleges still wanted him, but a full scholarship was off the table. Charlie, of course, was devastated, but there was nothing he was able to do.

Micah and Mack returned to college so they could finish out the semester, but due to their time away, their grades suffered. The good news, however, was they still managed to earn straight B's. Mr. Wade and Mr. Richardson returned to work after their leave, and Isabelle, for the first time, was free to live her life. She told the Aces to call her if they ever needed her assistance again. Finally, the archangels said their goodbyes as they ascended back to heaven but promised to return if they were needed.

Meanwhile, Ashmead was busy gathering all the new cryptids that Jason had created. He instructed them to stay put in the woods along the Georgia state line, where the remaining cryptids lived. The demon still planned to destroy the Aces, but first, he needed to reestablish order and find his new lead cryptid. Once he felt they were ready, his goal was to set them loose so they could finish killing the remaining Lobos. He decided to let Isabelle think she was truly free, but when the time was right, he planned to kill her too. He gave his word that he would not kill Toby, but he never said he couldn't torture her. Ashmead understood that if he was lucky, then an archangel could perish; however, he knew he had a better chance of tearing the Aces apart from within. The key to making that possible was convincing Tommy to help him. He left the cryptid camp and returned to hell as he laughed along the way.

The following weekend Micah asked Toby if she wanted to have dinner with him down on the beach. She replied, "Of course, what an excellent idea. Look at you trying to be creative and romantic at the same time." She told him that she would need to hunt first so she wouldn't be tempted to attack anyone down by the pier. He assured her that she would never go rogue and hurt another person.

Toby laughed as she told him, "I have urges to bite people every single day. The only thing that stops me from doing the unthinkable is you, Tommy, and all the other people in my life. If Isabelle still struggles every day, then how do you think I cope and handle myself? It is a daily struggle for me and also my biggest fear. Being a cryptid doesn't make you a monster; your behavior does. Do me a favor and please kill me if I ever lose complete control over my actions."

He promised her that he would honor her wish. She thanked him for respecting her wishes and told Micah she would see him later that evening.

Tommy was lying in bed, still thinking about all the events that had recently occurred. Even though he had killed Jason, he was dealing with a lot of anger, and he wasn't sure how to handle it. Tommy was angry that his sister was now a monster, upset about losing his mother and best friend, and extremely pissed off that he had lost the use of his right hand. He started to have resentment towards Micah, Isabelle, and all of the archangels. He felt torn between quitting the Aces or just going off and killing all the cryptids himself.

Tommy decided to talk with his dad and sister about what he was going through. Toby told him that nothing was his fault, and even though she was now a cryptid, she didn't blame him. His father advised him to take some time and let himself grieve before he did anything else. He yelled at his father saying, "I don't need to grieve! Grieving will not bring anyone back or turn my sister into a human again. I need to go and clear my head, staying here will only make me more insane."

Toby gave her brother a giant hug and reminded him that she would always be here for him. Tommy hugged her back as he said his goodbyes.

As Tommy drove off on his motorcycle, his only thought was to find and kill as many cryptids as possible.

He knew he wouldn't be fully satisfied until they were all dead, especially Isabelle. He remembered Isabelle telling everyone that she had led all the remaining cryptids south, so he at least had a starting point as he hopped onto Interstate 95. Once he drove into North Carolina, he realized everyone at the rest area was staring at him when they saw his hand. Tommy took his skull cap and placed it over his nub. He then wrapped duct tape around it before putting his jacket back on. He thought to himself, *Well now, maybe people will think I'm an injured veteran instead of a freak of nature.* The last thing he wanted during his crusade was to draw attention to himself. The best thing was to keep a low profile if he planned on being successful with his agenda.

Back in Virginia, Micah was driving to pick up Toby for their date. She was very excited to see Micah but told him she was preoccupied with thinking about her brother. He asked her what Tommy was thinking about when he went after the cryptids all by himself. She replied, "He's currently not thinking, but if I had tried to stop him, it would have made matters worse. You didn't see the look in his eyes; he is blaming himself for everything that has occurred over the past month." She asked Micah what he would have done differently.

He replied, "I have no idea, but I can see after all the current events your brother is not the same person. Regardless of how many cryptids he kills, if Ashmead chooses to, he can turn even more humans into servants."

Toby told Micah it was their job to help the cryptids, "If Isabelle and I can take a stand and do the right things, then so can the rest of us."

Micah replied, "That is wishful thinking, but we can give it a try."

The rest of their evening consisted of them getting appetizers, splitting a dinner, and walking along the shoreline. Once they reached the pier, Micah put his arm around her as he whispered in her ear, "I love you." They sat and watched the waves for a while then decided to continue walking on down the shore. The two of them eventually sat in the sand and started making out.

She looked at him, saying, "I want you, but I don't know if it is safe or wise to have sex. The more you get me excited, the harder it is for me to fight my urge to bite you, plus I'm afraid to know what would happen if we had intercourse."

Micah replied, "It's okay, just lay down with me, and I will hold you." Before long, they both fell asleep in each other's arms.

The next morning as the two love birds awoke; they found themselves staring at two officers. The cops asked if they were doing anything inappropriate and if they had been drinking. Micah replied, "No, officer, I guess we just fell asleep. Can you tell me what time it is?"

The officer told him that it was almost six in the morning, and it was time for them to leave.

Toby replied, "Of course, we do apologize. We were enjoying the sounds of the waves, and I guess the noise put us to sleep. Thank you for checking on us and making sure we were okay." The officer gave them their ID cards back as they headed to the parking lot.

Once they got to Micah's car, the two of them saw Isabelle waiting on them. She asked if she could ride with them because they needed to talk. Toby lifted the passenger seat as Isabelle got into the back seat. Before she told them why she came to see them, Toby asked her a question. She asked her if having sex was a good or bad idea.

Isabelle replied, "Well, you are technically a living-dead creature, so I'm going to say it's probably a bad idea. Can you get pregnant? I don't believe so, but I can't answer that question, honestly. One, I have never thought about it plus I was the only female cryptid for decades and have never had that question asked of me. The best advice I can give both of you is just to live your life and do what makes you happy. Now can we get down to the reason I came back to see the two of you?"

Micah replied, "Sure, go ahead; we are all ears."

Isabelle began by telling them, "Jason was a nuisance, but Ashmead is the one true threat. He is recruiting and training all the new cryptids that Jason had turned before his death. Freeing me was not by accident either, by releasing me now I do not have any influence over the cryptids. They will only listen and take orders from Ashmead, directly. Once their training is complete, he will release them to start attacking and creating chaos among the entire population. My guess is Ashmead will begin by attacking the Lobos and tracking Toby and me down.

"The outcome will be ugly, and my death is almost inevitable, but Toby doesn't have to experience the same fate. I would rather die fighting alongside my friends than live alone on the run for the rest of my life."

Micah replied, "You are not my friend; you are now family and have earned my respect. Let's go and get the others. We have some cryptids to kill."

# Chapter 16

As they were heading back to the apartment, Micah was debating whether or not to have Charlie help them. The semester was over for him and Mack, but his brother still had another month of school remaining, plus graduation. Isabelle told Micah that his brother should stay behind because he had been through enough in the past few weeks. Let him finish school and get his head clear before joining in on the crusade.

Toby replied, "I agree, but I think we need to track down Tommy and convince Adrian to help us as well. We really can't rely on the archangels because Michael will just tell us that we only defend and protect, and we never should initiate the fight. We all know when we wait, innocent people die."

Micah told the ladies to pause for a minute and suggested they talk to Charlie, Mack, Adrian, and Tommy, first. If there were no objections to them, then they would start with Mack.

They arrived at the apartment, and when Mack saw them together, he knew something was up. He said, "What is going on? Isabelle is here, so it can't be good."

Isabelle replied, "It's good to see you too, honey. I have only one question for you. Would you rather lead the charge or wait for the fight to come to you?"

He told her it was better to hit the problem head-on and then asked when they were planning to leave.

Micah replied, "Right after I've checked on my parents and talked to my brother. So grab your stuff, we are leaving soon."

As they arrived at the house, Mrs. Wade asked her son to stop pursuing the cryptids before someone else died. Isabelle replied, "People have already died, and more will continue to die if we don't act now. No one wants to end this war against the cryptids any more than me."

Before his mother could reply, Charlie came out of his room. He told his brother that he was ready and willing to join them. Micah told his brother that he needed to stay behind and finish school and protect their parents. He said, "It may take us months, maybe years to destroy all of the cryptids, you will have your opportunity to join in on the fight. I will call you once we truly need you." He then gave his brother a cell phone. "This is your graduation present from me, now please stay here and finish your senior year strong."

Charlie replied, "I will," and he hugged his brother and the ladies goodbye.

Once they got back in the car, Toby attempted to reach Tommy multiple times, but each time the call went straight to voicemail. Micah told everyone that they were heading south, and hopefully, at some point, they would find Adrian and Tommy along the way. "Hopefully, we will never walk into a situation blind ever again now that we have these bracelets."

Isabelle said, "Not unless we run into demons, then we will be in trouble."

Mack replied, "Well if that does occur, the archangels will come back for sure to help us."

Micah told his friend, "Whether the angels return or not, we must do our part and stop as many cryptids as possible. The longer we wait, the more Ashmead gets under our skin. Obviously, cryptids can choose their destiny, but if we don't show them there is another option, then we have failed them. It is not their fault. They are now monsters; killing them should always be our second option."

Meanwhile, Tommy was keeping tabs of all the cryptids he had encountered and killed. He was able to determine which ones were mature and who were newborns. The newborns moved faster, but they were careless as they attacked humans head-on. The older cryptids at least accumulated a plan of attack and tried to attack at night in abandoned areas. He was getting used to his new hand by either crushing skulls as he punched them or pinning them to the ground while cutting off their heads.

On his second night out, Tommy came across an entire pack of newborns. As he was killing them off, he realized he recognized one of them. The one in question was the young girl that Jason had possessed during the time of his death. He was confused because he assumed she had died since she was the vessel. What Tommy didn't know was Ashmead had turned her as she was taking her final breath. Once she saw Tommy, she fled into the woods, knowing she didn't have a chance in hell at defeating him.

He stopped in his tracks, not knowing what he should do next. Tommy was torn between killing and trying to help her. Finally, he decided to follow her trail right after he burned all the bodies. He knew it wasn't her fault, just like he never blamed Derek for his actions during the time he was possessed. He thought to himself, *Kayla must be Isabelle's replacement to lead his army.* Either way, Tommy was going to make sure that Kayla didn't get the opportunity to hurt another soul.

Kayla decided to return to camp so she could tell the others that the Aces were actively hunting them. Ashmead interrupted her and said, "Will you please shut up and stop complaining? I saved you so you could lead the cryptids, not run away from a fight. I could have let you die, but I didn't, and this is how you repay me?"

She replied, "No. I mean, yes. I mean, I don't know. I didn't ask to be a vessel or for you to save me."

The demon told her she became a vessel because she said yes to Jason, and no, she didn't ask to be saved, but if he had not saved her, then she wouldn't be standing here right now. Ashmead told her to go and kill Isabelle, and if she was successful, then she could return and lead the cryptids. She left knowing that either way, her life as she had known it was officially over. As she left and moved forward, her only options were to kill or be killed.

As Micah was driving, Toby instructed him to pull off to the side once she saw smoke coming from the woods. They all got out of the car and started walking toward the fire. As they got closer, Micah saw Tommy burning multiple bodies. He yelled at Micah to leave and go back home with his sister.

Toby replied, "We are not leaving, and you don't have to do this by yourself. You have already lost your hand, do you want to lose your life as well?"

Tommy told them that Ashmead had recruited hundreds, possibly even thousands of new cryptids, while also grooming Kayla to lead them.

Isabelle replied, "Kayla...are you sure? I guess that explains why he took her body. He must have turned her before she took her last breathe."

Getting extremely frustrated, Tommy agreed to go with them on one condition. He told everybody his only focus was to kill all the cryptids, so everyone better be on the same page. He told everyone that also included Isabelle.

Micah replied, "Yes, I agree with you. All cryptids must die except for Isabelle and Toby. Now let's go, we have some work to do."

Tommy gave Isabelle a look as he hopped on his bike. Toby told Isabelle that as long as she was with them, she would protect her from her brother.

She replied, "I appreciate that Toby, but we know someone is going to kill me eventually. It might as well be your brother; at least he will kill me quickly."

Several weeks later, the five of them had accounted for hundreds of cryptid deaths, but they knew they had just scratched the surface. Tommy wondered if Ashmead had finished training the newborns or if he was still out creating new ones. He thought for every cryptid they killed; there were two more just around the corner. He told Micah they could be doing this for the rest of their life, and it wouldn't matter unless they were able to kill Ashmead.

He replied, "Jason, Ashmead, it doesn't matter who dies. There will always be demons turning humans into cryptids. For all we know, Lucifer and other demons could be turning people into monsters too." He told Tommy he would be heading back home toward the end of the week so he could attend Charlie's graduation. He asked if he wanted to wait for him to return or continue on the hunt without him. Tommy told Micah to take his sister with him, and he would go on with Mack and Isabelle. Tommy promised his friend he wouldn't kill her while he was gone. He told Micah to take his motorcycle back while he drove his car. By the end of the week, Micah and Toby hugged their friends goodbye, telling them they would catch up with everyone next week.

Isabelle looked at Tommy and told him she would take the first watch, but first, she needed to hunt before she lost complete control. He said, "I don't trust you to take watch over us. I will stay up instead."

She replied, "You can barely keep your eyes open. Now, if you don't get some rest, then you will be no good in a fight. Do you want to become an easy target for the newborns?" She told him to trust her because she no longer had any ties to cryptids or the demons, plus she saved his sister from dying. "What else do I need to prove and show you I am here to help?" Before Tommy had the opportunity to reply Mack told him to shut up and go to sleep. Tommy glared at both of them as he lay across the back seat, trying to fall asleep.

Meanwhile, Ashmead continued training the newborns and was becoming extremely impatient about it. He had zero tolerance for the cryptids that kept playing and fooling around. They started focusing once Ashmead killed several of them. He thought to himself, *If I can't build my army through leadership, then I will rule by fear.* He already had Kayla out tracking down Isabelle, a small group searching for the new Lobo's camp, and sent several hundred cryptids back to Virginia to attack the Aces. The demon had no idea they were already out hunting and killing off his recruits. He thought if he was able to eliminate all of their allies, then Micah and the other Aces may relinquish their powers.

As they pulled into the driveway, Charlie and his parents were surprised to see Micah and Toby. His mother asked if they had destroyed all the cryptids. He told her they had not, but she could rest easier knowing they did kill several hundred of them. Charlie said, "I can't believe you came back just for me. What you and the others are doing is much more important than my stupid graduation."

Micah replied, "Nothing is more important than family, I mean absolutely nothing, so please stop your nonsense. If you want to join us later when we continue our crusade, then you are more than welcome to come." He told his brother that his bag was already packed and ready to go. Toby asked him how he was feeling. Charlie said to her that he had both good and bad days. "It was tough not thinking about his time in the cage, but the memories also helped to keep me motivated and focused. Enough about me, I'm sure the two of you are hungry and could use a hot shower."

Toby hugged everyone and said, "Yes, you are so right. The first shower is mine," as she walked down the hall toward the bathroom.

The next day was all about celebrating Charlie's big day. He was finally graduating from high school, and his day was overwhelmed with mixed emotions. He was ready to start college in the fall and play ball at the state university. He was torn between college and his obligations to the other Aces, especially his brother. Micah told his brother that if he wanted to have both, then they would find a way. Right now, he asked Charlie to just focus on today and be ready to walk down the aisle when they called his name. Micah told him that they would worry about everything else later. Charlie asked Toby how he looked in his brand new suit.

She replied, "You are extremely handsome; it's too bad. I'm already dating your brother."

He replied, "Thank you, I appreciate the compliment." Charlie's dad walked back into the house and asked if everyone was ready.

Mrs. Wade replied, "I am ready to go, just not ready to see my last baby graduate."

Micah glared at his mom, saying, "Come on, mom, and please don't embarrass Charlie today. He is already turning red, and he hasn't even gotten his diploma yet."

The university gymnasium was packed with people as the entire city was using it for their high school graduations. As soon as one school finished, they were getting the gym ready for the next one. Micah asked Toby if she was okay being around all these people. She kept assuring him that she was fine, and if anything changed, she would remove herself from the ceremony. After sitting for a solid hour, the principal finally called Charlie's name. Not only was he awarded his diploma, but he had earned honor roll and a plaque stating he was the top athlete of the year. After the ceremony, the family waited for Charlie to come outside so they could congratulate him, but before they could, they were under the attack of dozens of cryptids.

# Chapter 17

Once they got outside, Micah and Toby realized that the cryptids were surrounding the auditorium. Micah created force fields to protect everyone that was standing around while trying to draw the cryptids inside. A few minutes later, Micah instructed his brother to get everyone a safe location. Toby was fighting them off the best she could, and Micah was concentrating on keeping everyone safe under his protective force field. When it seemed as if the creatures would overpower them, Adrian showed up to provide more assistance.

Micah shouted to his friend, "I am glad to see you, buddy, perfect timing as always."

He replied, "Of course, no problem! I wouldn't miss my friend's graduation for anything, but he didn't mention there would be an after-party." Once everyone was safely secured, he yelled for his friends to get behind him. He drew the electricity from the outlets around him and channeled it toward the cryptids frying all of them in the process. Adrian yelled out to Micah, "You can control electricity, too? Next time why don't you lead with that?"

He just laughed and said, "Let's go, Charlie. Please get us out of here."

Back at the house, Mrs. Wade was still freaking out over what happened after the ceremony. Micah attempted to calm his mom down by telling her that it was time for everyone to stuff their faces and watch Charlie unwrap his gifts. Mrs. Wade asked her son after she had finally calmed down if he was still planning on hunting more cryptids. He replied, "Yes, I have to, it is my obligation. When we are not hunting them, then they start to hunt us. I will not put you and everyone else within the community in jeopardy."

Micah knew that his mother worried, but he took on this responsibility, and now he must do whatever it takes to protect the individuals he loved. He was torn on whether or not he wanted his brother to join in on the fight but knew if he denied him the opportunity, then he would join out of spite. Charlie thanked everyone for coming and for all the lovely gifts. Everyone hugged him as Micah replied, "You are welcome big guy." He then said, "We all better get some rest because tomorrow we are back to doing what we do best, hunting down and killing cryptids."

The following morning, Toby rode off with Micah while Adrian left with Charlie riding shotgun in his brand new truck. Adrian asked his friend if he believed he could be an Ace and still live a normal life. He replied, "I hope so, my ultimate dream is to play professional baseball after finishing college. Schools are looking to give me a full scholarship, and teams are asking to sign me right after graduation. Of course, that was before I abandoned the team and missed the last two games." He asked Adrian if there would ever be a day when he and other Lobos could live in peace.

He replied, "Probably not, I don't ever see my people living in harmony. If it's not the cryptids or the demons, then I'm sure somebody out there will still display hatred or want us dead. You know what we do is extremely hard, especially when most of society does not know we exist or if they did, they probably wouldn't appreciate us anyway. Regardless of the outcome, this is who we are now. The bottom line is we can never stop fighting and doing what is right."

Charlie asked Adrian how the other Lobos were holding up since they were forced to leave their community.

Adrian told his young friend, "Home is where your heart is, but starting over is tough for anyone. The elders feel as if they failed everyone by not protecting their people, and the kids are scared and worried about the unknown future." He then explained how he felt torn between helping the others re-build their new lives and being there for him and the other Aces.

Charlie asked him if he felt responsible for their safety and well-being.

Adrian replied, "No, I don't feel that helping you is my responsibility. However, I see you and the others as not only my allies but also my friends. We both have the same common enemies, and if one of us fails, then we both will lose. If that ever occurs, then that would be the end for you, me, and the entire human race. Now drive faster before your brother leaves us behind."

Heading down the interstate, Toby told Micah that if it wasn't for Adrian's help, yesterday could have ended very differently. He acknowledged her while saying, "Yes, I am extremely grateful that he was there, but I'm even more ecstatic that no one was injured or killed. The biggest concern right now is stopping all the newborns, but we also need to find Ashmead as well. It doesn't matter how many we kill if the demons keep turning more and more humans into cryptids. Ashmead has to be planning something big. If we can figure out what his plan is, then maybe we can end him as well. It sounds like we have a starting point; but first, we need to locate Tommy and the others."

Toby grabbed her phone, so she could call her brother and was surprised when he answered his phone right away. The first thing he asked about was Charlie's graduation and if they were already on their way.

She replied, "Well, let's just say graduation was exciting and action-packed. It is probably best if we tell you about those events in person, and yes, we grabbed breakfast this morning and have been on the road ever since." She informed her brother that Adrian and Charlie were also traveling with them.

He replied, "That is awesome news! We could use all the help we can get right now. For all we know, there could be tens of thousands of cryptids along the way. Ashmead's ultimate goal is to eliminate not only all the Lobos but the Aces as well. At some point, we are going to need the archangels to return because we can't do this alone." He jokingly told his sister, "I only have one good hand left, and I'm not planning on losing it."

After hanging up with Toby, He told Mack and Isabelle to continue tracking cryptids until they got to the next rest stop. He told them they could always crash there and get some sleep.

Mack replied, "Hell no, we have slept the last two nights in the car; we all need a good night's sleep and a hot shower."

Tommy looked at him, saying, "Fine, we will get a room, but the bitch can sleep with you. I would hate to have another reason to kill her."

She replied, "Yes, you want me dead I get it, but do not call me the 'B' word. You do realize your sister would be dead right now if it weren't for me. She is the only human I have ever turned, and I did it so you and Micah wouldn't have to grieve her, so please go screw yourself."

Mack interrupted their conversation, telling them to shut the hell up. He told Tommy, "Out of all the cryptids, Isabelle should be the last one you need to worry about. Now, let's check this one last strip of woods so we can finally retire for the night."

As the three of them were walking through the woods, they encountered only a few cryptids. Mack asked Isabelle if she thought they were going into hiding because they were afraid to die.

She replied, "I'm sure the newborns are scared because whether they are being hunted by us or dying, they know they are disobeying Ashmead. Either way, they don't have a choice in the matter."

Mack yelled out to Tommy, "I sense there is something else out here with us, but I don't see any more cryptids."

He replied, "Keep your eyes open and never ignore your gut. I know for a fact my instincts are never wrong." What the guys didn't realize was their gut was warning them of someone else out there in the woods watching them. About a hundred yards out, Kayla was busy tracking them and was hot on their trail. She was waiting for a vulnerable time to attack. Isabelle could sense something else was near but had no idea it was Kayla or the fact she was hunting her and not the Aces. Finally, all of them agreed to leave and stop at the first decent hotel they could find.

Tommy drove a few more miles down the road and finally saw an exit with a Holiday Inn. He told the other two that he was getting off the ramp, and one of them was paying for the room. Mack replied, "I knew you would say that. It's fine, I will get us a room with two beds on the first floor."

Isabelle walked in with him and whispered in his ear, "Get a room in the back of the hotel. I have a feeling something was following us on the way in. Plus, if your friend does anything stupid, then hopefully no one will see it if we are in the rear of the building." He acknowledged her as he asked the front desk clerk for a bottom floor rear room.

The clerk looked at Mack, saying, "The two of you make a cute couple, here is a DO NOT DISTURB sign to hang on your door."

Isabelle replied, "Thank you very much, ma'am," as she grabbed Mack's hand and said, "Come on, babe, it's time for us to lose our clothes and enjoy each other."

He put his arm around her as they walked away, saying, "Very funny. Amazing performance by the way."

She looked directly at him and just winked, "No problem, babe. Anytime!"

As they walked toward the car, Tommy asked why the two of them were smiling. Isabelle looked at him, saying,

"Wouldn't you like to know, but a lady never kisses and tells."

He looked at Mack, saying, "Very funny, but I know you are not that stupid to be messing around with her."

He asked Tommy to chill out, and please grab the bags because she is just messing with him.

He replied, "Fine, but I'm not grabbing her stuff, plus I call the first shower." Mack just shook his head and thought no matter what Isabelle says or does for them, Tommy will never change his mind about her. Once they were settled in their room, Mack offered to walk next store and pick up a pizza for everyone.

While Mack was grabbing dinner and Tommy was getting cleaned up, Isabelle decided to go down the hall to get some sodas and fill up their ice bucket. As she was getting change out of her pocket, she was attacked by Kayla from behind. She scratched Isabelle multiple times as she held onto her hair. Isabelle threw herself back against the wall trying to break free from Kayla's grip. They exchanged blows and ended up wrestling each other onto the floor. Kayla reached for the knife that she had in her back pocket.

Once Isabelle saw her reaching for a weapon, she bit her arm, trying to get her to drop it. Kayla fought through the pain as she still managed to stab her in the shoulder blade. As soon as she was stuck, Isabelle screamed out in pain when Mack heard it from a distance. He ran back to the rear of the hotel and saw Kayla on top of Isabelle. He knocked her off of his friend, and as the newborn went to charge at him, he chopped off her head, killing her instantly.

Isabelle got up, holding her shoulder as she hugged and thanked him for saving her life. They carried the dead body out in the woods and then poured buckets of water on the sidewalk rinsing the blood away. He walked her back to the room; then went to the front desk to ask if they had a first-aid kit. The clerk asked if everything was alright.

He replied, "Yes, everything is fantastic. My adorable girlfriend tripped walking into the room and has a cut and bump on her head. I have already kissed her forehead, and now I just need to put a bandage on it." She handed him some ointment, bandages, and extra washcloths and told him that he was a loving boyfriend. As he was walking away, she told him to be safe and enjoy the rest of his evening. He thanked her for her hospitality as he headed back to his room.

As soon as Isabelle walked into the room, Tommy asked who had tried to kill her this time. She replied, "You are such dick, but if you must know it was Kayla. Somehow she survived back when you killed Jason. That would have only been possible if Ashmead turned her seconds after you stabbed her. Which would make sense now on why he took her body once he disappeared that day."

He told her that he was glad to see that she survived the attack.

Extremely confused, she asked, "You're glad I'm okay?"

He replied, "Yes, of course, it would have pissed me off if someone else had killed you, and it wasn't me."

She shook her head, saying, "As I said before, you are truly a dick."

Seconds later, Mack walked back in and asked Isabelle to sit down. He told Tommy to grab some slices of pizza while it's still hot, and he would eat after patching her up.

He properly cleaned and stitched up her wound. She looked at Mack and thanked him for being so kind and for not asking her to remove her bra. He laughed, saying, "I'm sure you look amazing topless, but it's not the time or place to get fresh with each other." After he was done, he told her that he had taped a piece of the plastic over the bandage, and she was safe to take a shower without it getting wet. He said to her that he would get one after her and promised to save her some pizza.

As she walked into the bathroom, Tommy just glared at Mack with a disgusted look. He asked the love doctor if they should be worried about the backlash from killing Kayla. He looked at Tommy and said, "Really, backlash, we will forever be looking over our shoulder until all the cryptids are dead. However, you may be correct. Kayla was Isabelle's replacement, so killing her will truly piss off Ashmead to no means."

Tommy told him that he would take the first watch while they tried to get some rest, "It is probably best that we stick around this area until Micah and the others arrive in the morning."

# Chapter 18

The next morning as the time was drawing near for everyone to check out, Micah and the rest of the gang finally arrived. The group embraced each other and was happy to see everyone was safe and still alive. Isabelle said, "I'm a little banged up right now, but thanks to Mack, I will survive." Toby wanted to know how she got injured and asked if it was her brother. She replied, "No, it wasn't your brother, even though he has told me multiple times he still plans to kill me." Toby slapped her brother in the back of the head, telling him once more to leave Isabelle alone, "She is on our side, plus she's my friend."

Tommy replied, "Okay, I will stop with my remarks, but please don't let your guard down; she is still a cryptid."

She told her brother in a straightforward tone, "So am I. Now please, we need to break down the last two weeks for everyone so we can decide our next plan of action."

While Tommy was filling them in, Isabelle walked over to talk to Charlie and Adrian. She congratulated him on finishing school and told him that he was still cute. Isabelle said, "Be careful when you go off to college. Don't let any of those party girls trip you up." She asked Adrian how the pack was doing and wanted to know how long he was sticking around this time.

He replied, "Honestly, I have no idea. I was just planning to attend the graduation, but we fell under attack by hundreds of cryptids right after the ceremony. I will help where I can, but you already know my true alliance falls with my fellow Lobos. Come on, let's see everyone so we know what's going on because I would hate for us not to be on the same page."

Seconds later, Michael appeared in front of everyone. He told the Aces that Ashmead was releasing his new cryptids among the people in numerous directions. He warned them that Kayla was chosen as the new leader, and his priorities were to kill Isabelle and to eliminate the rest of the Lobos.

Mack replied, "We already know about Kayla, and she is no longer an issue. I killed her last night, even though she was almost successful at killing Isabelle."

Isabelle told everyone that Ashmead would never stop until Toby and she are dead, "He hates the fact I am no longer his slave, and no matter what, Toby will never follow him. She would rather die than live a damned life."

Adrian said, "Well, if he is sending creatures to attack my people, then it's time for me to leave now."

Charlie replied, "We are not going to let you go on a suicide mission all alone. I volunteer to go with you."

Michael told the Aces that they were stronger together, but splitting up is the only way to fight them all. "This is what Ashmead wants, so we need to put an end to his madness." The archangel told Adrian and Charlie to go and informed them Raphael was already there waiting. As

Charlie was getting ready to teleport Adrian back home, Isabelle informed him that she was coming too.

Micah requested to talk with Michael alone and asked him where the other archangels were and why had he not come sooner. He told Micah that Uriel and Gabriel were trying to track down Ashmead, and they were dealing with something else of high importance. The hierarchy didn't want to tell the young Ace that the other archangels had been following Tommy because they feared he was being influenced by Ashmead or even Lucifer himself. The angel advised the Aces and Toby to continue tracking down cryptids, and if they encountered any demons, he would return.

He told Michael they needed to focus on destroying Ashmead or the chaos would never end. He informed Micah that killing the head demon was just as tricky as destroying an archangel, "It is not impossible, but hard to do. Even if we can destroy him, the devil would only appoint another demon. Regardless, I do hear and agree with you; he will eventually show us his ugly face."

Several weeks before, when the angels had ascended back to heaven, they felt a terrible revelation was about to unfold. Not only did they think the worst was yet to come, but they also questioned themselves on selecting four Aces instead of just one. The main reason behind Michael's decision was he never wanted another Ace to get injured as Victor did. The second reason was they all knew the world was getting worse, and they needed as much help as possible. He never agreed with Micah about choosing his team, but he had no choice because he needed him to lead them.

Michael thought Mack was too afraid and would fold under pressure; Charlie was too young and probably would get someone killed; and Tommy, because he never would listen. However, Uriel had other reasons why they should worry about Tommy. He told Michael that taking his dagger was stupid, but the look in his eyes when he grabbed it was utterly indescribable. He told the other archangels how for a split second, his eyes had turned black, and ever since, Uriel had been keeping a close eye on him.

Michael couldn't explain why his eyes had turned black. He only knew he had seen a person's eyes turn black once before. When the other archangels asked when that happened, Michael told them it was right before God cast Lucifer out of heaven. He told them how black eyes represent pure hatred and evil of the highest level; he asked Uriel once more if he was a hundred percent certain Tommy's eyes had turned black.

He replied, "Yes, I am sure. You can never forget an experience so completely and utterly profound." After he heard those words, he ordered Uriel and Gabriel to follow Tommy from a distance, "But he must never know you are watching him."

Raphael asked Michael what they were planning to do next. He replied, "We will remain in heaven until they are all back together again. Once that occurs, you will return and locate the Lobos, and I will make myself known to the Aces. Together we will declare war on the cryptids before Ashmead recruits any more creatures for his army. Just remember, we must never tell the Aces about what Uriel saw. There is still a possibility, things could unfold differently because the fact remained Tommy will always have a choice to choose between good and evil. Our job is to be ready and act based upon his final decision."

Meanwhile, back in the forest, Adrian and the others were welcomed by Raphael as soon as they arrived. He told Adrian that he was waiting for him to get there because he knew the elders would not allow him to let him step onto their land. He replied, "It's okay. I'm here, come on and follow me." Delisle's most trusted advisor stated the archangel may pass, but not the nasty ass cryptid. He told his advisor that Isabelle was an ally, and if he trusted her, then she was allowed in. The elder gave Adrian a dirty look as he moved aside to let her enter. He asked the elders to gather everyone together because he needed to speak to his people. A few minutes later, he was formerly addressing his fellow Lobos, both young and old.

The first thing Adrian wanted to mention was how much he cared about and loved everyone. He told them that the time had finally come for them to take a stand and fight. He explained to everyone that the cryptids and possibly even Ashmead were heading their way. He thought instead of staying put and getting ambushed by their enemy; they would spread out and bring the fight to them. The element of surprise is a powerful tactic, and it may be the difference between them winning or losing this war. He thought it was wise to ask the teenagers to go with Charlie so they would be safe.

One of the youngsters spoke up and said, "We are tired of running, the elders have been training us, and we are ready to fight beside you." The kid told Adrian, along with everyone else, "Life is not worth living if we survive, and the rest of you die." The young Lobo looked around as he announced that the youngsters were no longer helpless kids.

The head elder also looked at Adrian, saying, "Don't worry; we are all ready to follow your lead. We will be ready to move out at dawn."

Charlie looked at Isabelle and said, "Wow! The Lobos are truly accepting him as their new king. I think that is wonderful; he is ready to be their leader."

She poked Charlie in the side, telling him he had come a long way, and if he ever mastered his teleporting abilities, then he could become the greatest Ace of all time.

He asked her, "What are you talking about?"

She glared at him, saying, "You know…your ability to teleport people or demons straight to hell."

He asked how she knew about his powers. She replied, "You don't exist for over two hundred years and not learn the way of the Aces. The problem is no Ace in my lifetime has ever successfully traveled to hell and return." Before he could reply, she grabbed his face and kissed him. Stunned, he said, "Why did you just kiss me?"

"I forgot to get you a present, so I thought a kiss would do. Don't get too excited though, you are way too young for me, besides I gave my heart away a lifetime ago."

The following morning Charlie, Isabelle, and the Lobos gathered their personal belongings together as they were preparing to head out. Adrian asked all the youngsters to stay in the middle as the elders formed a barrier around them. He and Raphael led the way as Charlie and Isabelle were bringing in the rear. The archangel instructed them to kill any creature with yellow eyes, and he would take care of any demons that crossed their path.

Isabelle yelled out among the group, "Kill anything with yellow eyes except for me." She told the archangel to be careful what they say, "Because they are ready to pounce on me."

Raphael replied, "Sorry, the female cryptids are the only exceptions to my rule. Now let's go, we have a lot of ground to cover."

As they were heading out, Adrian gave Charlie one of his warrior blades. He told him since his abilities didn't put him in a position to fight, he thought he could use something to protect himself. He thanked his friend for the weapon as he reached down to grab his backpack. He told Charlie, "If things get worse, please promise you will get as many of my people as possible to safety."

He replied, "I promise, but don't worry, we have the upper hand because they will be caught off guard."

He told his young friend, "Please don't get too cocky. Anything can happen, so please, always be alert and ready to go."

Isabelle was telling Charlie that she never thought it would get this bad. She was conflicted because she wanted to help the other cryptids, but she realized they were beyond help. The creatures were nothing more than slaves to the demons, and the only way to set them free was to eliminate them. She knew if they were successful, then she could finally rest in peace. The one thing Isabelle struggled with regarding that outcome was she could convince one of her friends to kill her. But for now, her mission was to stay alive and focus on the task at hand.

Charlie had numerous thoughts running through his head as everyone was walking through the woods. He wondered if he would be able to live a normal life. Would he have enough time for his studies and his teammates on the baseball team? He also wondered if they found a way to kill all the cryptids, would everyone make it out alive. He thought whatever happened, it was his job to protect everyone and make sure they were guaranteed to see another day.

Until these last few months, Charlie was only close to his family and maybe some of his teammates. Now he felt close to his family, the other Aces, Toby, Isabelle, the archangels, Adrian and the rest of the Lobos, along with the rest of humanity. He was starting to feel the weight of the world on his shoulders, and his only thought was, *Would he be able to handle it all when the time came?*

# Chapter 19

Michael had returned to heaven, hoping to get a report from the other angels. Both Uriel and Gabriel told the hierarchy that Tommy still had a lot of built-up anger. However, he was currently taking his anger out by killing as many cryptids he could get his hands on. The angel thought Ashmead strongly influenced Tommy, but it was too soon to tell if the effects were going to be positive or negative.

There had not been any evidence of Ashmead or any other demon persuading him to go dark. Uriel also told Michael that he had not seen his eyes turn black since the day he killed Jason. The hierarchy told the other archangels it was all good news but ordered them to keep observing him. He told his fellow angels that Tommy and the other Aces should already be out tracking down more cryptids. Michael advised the angels to continue following Tommy but to keep their distance unless the demons show up or he starts to turn evil.

The hierarchy remained in heaven as he wanted to consult with the Lord and get His advice on their plans. God spoke to Michael and informed him to stay the course. The Lord said, "For I know what the future will hold, what has happened will pass and what will occur will also pass. I love all my children, which is why I gave them free will and the opportunity to make their own choices. My children have to make that choice for themselves, but just like Lucifer, some will decide not to follow me."

Michael replied, "Uriel witnessed Tommy's eyes turning black. That can't be a good sign of things to come."

The Lord instructed Michael once again to look after his children, aka the Aces, and continue to guide them in the right direction. If Tommy chooses to follow down the dark path, then he will be judged by his heavenly father, accordingly.

Meanwhile, Micah and the others were traveling through South Carolina on Interstate 95, when several dozen cryptids greeted them. Tommy yelled to his friend to keep his sister close as he and Mack ran toward the creatures. The two of them killed the cryptids by crushing their skulls and cutting off their heads. Micah felt helpless as he could only protect himself using his force field ability as there was no electricity to draw from at the moment. Toby had her boyfriend covered as she decapitated any cryptids that got close to him.

As she was fighting them, one of the creatures knocked her on her back. Micah immediately grabbed a tree branch as he hit the cryptid off her. He trapped the creature within a force field then suddenly sneezed, which caused the barrier shut, killing the cryptid instantly. Toby looking extremely confused, asked, "How in the hell did you do that?"

He replied, "I have no idea; the only thing I did was sneeze."

She yelled out to him, "Wait, it wasn't you sneezing; it was your eyes blinking that caused it." She tossed another one toward him, asking him to do the same thing. He trapped the cryptid once more than blinked his eyes, which resulted in the same outcome. The force crushed the creature causing its body to explode.

She winked at him, saying, "Awesome, new power. Just don't blink around me." He laughed as they killed the remaining cryptids.

As everyone was gathering the dead bodies, Micah asked Toby if she remembered the area Isabelle took her to after she was turned. She replied, "Yes, I remember the area very well. Don't worry; I will be able to find it again. It is near the Florida/Georgia state line."

Tommy shouted, "Well, that is great news; at least we know we are headed in the right direction."

Mack asked if they were going to just leave the bodies stacked on one another in the middle of the woods. Micah replied, "Well, if we leave them and someone finds the bodies, then there will be heat on us and a lot of questions. However, if we burn the bodies as we have in the past, then we will be drawing attention to ourselves from everyone, including the cryptids." Even though Mack volunteered to stay behind and contain the fire, his friend Micah ordered him to keep going. He instructed everyone that he would be the one to stay back and contain the fire. He asked the others to keep moving forward, and he would eventually catch up to them.

Micah stayed until all the bodies were destroyed, and the fire had burned out. As he was trying to leave, cops and firefighters arrived on the scene. Micah escaped by traveling further into the woods as he headed south. After walking several miles, he finally came out of the woods and started to move along the edge of the road. Minutes later, a van drove up next to him, and a voice told him to get in. Noticing it was Victor, he decided to get into the vehicle. Once Micah shut the door, Victor told him that they needed to talk. He told him not to worry; he promised he was heading in the same direction as his friends. Micah saw the look in Victor's eyes and knew whatever he needed to tell him was very important. As Victor got back on the road, he instructed Micah to buckle his seat belt as he headed down the road.

He told Micah to listen up because he needed to tell him the truth behind the archangels and demons. Victor informed his young friend that Ashmead was just a puppet to Lucifer, just like Jason. The current ranking order is Lucifer, aka Satan, then a demon named Dagon followed by Ashmead, then it was his stooge, Jason. Micah looked at him, utterly confused. Victor said, "In the beginning, before God created everything, he formed angels in heaven. As you already know, just like most humans Lucifer disobeyed God and was cast out of heaven. The devil may have been the only archangel cast out that day, but he also had five other angels who fell with him."

He replied, "The Bible talks about other angels following Lucifer that day, but their names were never mentioned."

Victor told him, "The other angels cast out that day were, Moloch, Chenosh, Beliai, Beelzebub, and Dagon. Shortly after they fell, they challenged the archangels for supremacy. Michael, Raphael, Gabriel, and Uriel destroyed each of them, leaving only Dagon behind. Since he followed Lucifer and did not challenge the angels, Lucifer appointed him the king of hell over all the other demons. Once that occurred, Dagon handpicked Ashmead to be his first-in-command. My thoughts are one day, Dagon will get tired of Ashmead acting like he is in charge and most likely will end him. It upset the angels to kill their former brothers, but they didn't have a choice."

He asked Victor why he decided to tell him about all of this now. He replied, "When push comes to shove, I wonder if the archangels will be up for the task to destroy more of their former friends. I feel the reason I am in this wheelchair is that Michael hesitated to kill Dagon twenty-five years ago. It was a low-level demon who attacked me, but it was Dagon who gave the order, not Ashmead. The king of hell vanished as soon as he witnessed Michael stabbing the fellow demon. If the angels can stop Ashmead and Dagon, then it will also end the reign of the cryptids forever."

He asked Victor how he knew all of this information. He told Micah that he studied religion in college and read a lot on angelology. He said, "So that makes you an expert, or are you just full of it?"

Victor replied, "Ask Michael about it if you don't believe me. When I approached him about this after my accident, he confirmed that everything I said was true. However, he did refuse to go into any detail with me about it. It is your choice if you choose to believe me or not, but just remember angels can't lie. So if Michael confirms my story, then it must be true.?"

Micah told Victor that he had no reason not to believe him. He said, "This changes everything. We need to focus our attention on finding the demons."

Victor replied, "No, you and the others have to kill as many cryptids as possible first, or you will never get near Ashmead. You better hope that an archangel shows up immediately if you or the other Aces do locate a demon. If not, then you will encounter the same fate as me or worse, you could be killed unless you want to be like your friend and lose your hand by touching their dagger. What Tommy did was not heroic; it was completely and utterly stupid even though he did destroy a demon. So please take my advice and approach this battle as if it may be your last." He then pulled the car off to the side and informed Micah that his friends were up ahead. He thanked Victor for helping him as he got out of the vehicle. He shook Micah's hand and wished him luck.

Micah eventually caught up with his friends and told them there was something he needed to say. Mack asked if everything was okay and had something happened after they left him. He told everyone after he burned the bodies, he had to wait for the firefighters to leave. Once it was safe to move forward, someone driving by flagged him down. "It was Victor who stated he needed to talk to me. As we were riding along, he informed me there was another demon more powerful than Ashmead that we should be worried about." Micah said, "Ashmead is nothing more than a pawn, just like Jason. The true king of hell is a demon named Dagon. Victor informed me the only way to stop the cryptids is to destroy both demons. Dagon was one of the six angels God had cast out of heaven. The archangels killed four of them shortly afterward, leaving just Lucifer and Dagon."

Tommy looked at his friend like he was crazy. He said, "What…Come again, please tell me you are messing with us."

Micah replied, "I wish I were joking, but I have absolutely no reason not to trust Victor. We all need to have a long talk with Michael once we see him again."

# Chapter 20

Elsewhere, the Lobos, along with their friends, continued searching for any cryptids in the surrounding areas. Adrian called out to Charlie and informed him to yell out if he picks up a presence of any kind. He told him so far everything seemed to be quiet, but he would let him know if anything changed. Isabelle looked over at Charlie and requested one of the Aces, presumably not Tommy, kills her once this is over. He replied, "Stop talking like that. You have not given us any reason to harm or kill you."

She told him, "If they do find a way to stop Ashmead and the other cryptids, then everything will never be finished unless Toby and I are killed as well."

He turned his head, saying, "I hear you, but I'm not comfortable killing either one of you. You should know Micah and Tommy will never allow anyone to hurt Toby."

Isabelle replied, "I understand, I truly do, but to permanently end the reign of cryptids forever, we all must die. Toby and I are not an exception to that rule. Just think about it, that is all I'm saying for now." Charlie acknowledged her as they kept walking through the woods.

Adrian continued to lead with Raphael by his side. The archangel told Adrian how much he had grown since the passing of his father. The angel said, "I know you and your dad had different leadership skills, but the one thing both of you shared was your undying love and devotion for your people. The other archangels and I were wrong to think the Lobos only had one purpose. My purpose has always been the same as yours: To love and assist everyone in need. You and your people have lost so much, but yet here you are, leading them into battle. Why don't you lead everyone away from here and start over."

Adrian replied, "Yes, it's true. I am not a fan of angels, but we all want the same thing, and the Aces are not only my friends, I also think of them as members of my family. The bottom line is we can't destroy all the evil in the world, but we can end the terror that evil has created. If we can successfully end the cryptids, then maybe my people can live a normal life."

The elder Lobo was getting tired, and the youngsters were starting to get restless, so Adrian ordered his people to start setting up camp for the night. Raphael instructed Adrian and Charlie to get some rest too, and he and Isabelle would take first watch. The angel told Isabelle that just because Ashmead had set her free didn't mean he was finished with her. She nodded her head, "Yes, I know. It feels like I am forever looking over my shoulders and constantly living in fear, which is getting old. Do you recommend Charlie or Adrian kill me now? We both know I am not promised a happy ending."

Raphael told her that convincing them to kill her now would be tough, especially since she had gained their trust. She replied, "Yes, tell me about it. Charlie has already told me that he could not kill me. It is too bad angels are forbidden to kill humans or any creatures that may look like one. My fate will probably lie in the hands of Ashmead or Tommy. If that does occur, then my life will end in pure misery."

Before Charlie went to sleep, he called his brother to give him an update. He told Micah that they had been searching all day and did not encounter one single cryptid. Micah confirmed they had killed an entire pack of cryptids earlier that morning, but it had been quiet ever since. Charlie recommended they all come back together again, and Micah assured him they were covering more ground separately.

He also told his brother about his conversation with Isabelle. He told him if they were successful in killing all of the cryptids and Ashmead, then the girls must die too. Charlie explained how if just one cryptid lived, then there would always be the possibility they could start over again.

Micah replied, "I understand what Isabelle is saying, but Toby's death will not be an option. Tommy, and I will never let that happen. Unless there is something else we need to discuss, then I am going to let you go and say good-bye."

He replied, "No, that is all for now. Please be safe my brother I will talk to you again soon."

Charlie tried to lie down and go to sleep, but he sensed something terrible was about to happen. He was convinced he attracted the cryptids wherever he went. He thought back to the baseball game, his neighborhood, and of course, the day of his high school graduation. His biggest fear wasn't dying; it was not being able to protect and keep his family safe. Charlie knew if he were able to fall asleep, then it would only be for a few hours at best. Ever since Jason had him locked up in the cage, he had a difficult time sleeping and staying asleep because being in a cage still played games with his mind. He wanted to talk to Isabelle about it, but he knew she was probably fighting with her own demons from her time in the cage. Charlie wanted nothing more than to capture Ashmead in the same cage and drop it in the pits of hell. Then maybe, just maybe, he would be able to once again sleep at night.

The next morning everyone was up and ready to go at the crack of dawn. Charlie got up and asked why they were leaving so early. Adrian replied, "You are with us now. Lobos go to bed extremely late, and we are up super early. Come on, let's go sleeping beauty, sleeping is for the weak."

He yelled back, "No, sleeping is for us humans who can't function without it."

Isabelle walked by both of them, saying, "Boys stop arguing before I bite both of you. If you ask me sleeping is highly overrated."

"Charlie jokingly asked what Adrian would become if you did bite him."

Before she could reply, he said, "One much-decapitated cryptid, and it wouldn't be pretty."

She glared at Adrian, saying, "Thanks, babe, love you too!"

Raphael just looked at everyone, saying, "If you children are done bickering, then we can head out."

As they were walking, a cryptid jumped down from a tree and surrendered to them. He requested to see Isabelle and told them he wasn't there to harm anyone. Adrian being very cautious agreed to the cryptid's request under one condition. He told him he could speak to her in his presence only. The cryptid agreed as the three of them walked away from the others. Adrian said to him that he had exactly three minutes to tell them what he needed to say.

First, he asked Isabelle how she had obtained her freedom and how he could do the same. Second, he told them there was a new demon handing out orders, and he was scarier than Ashmead. Finally, he asked if she would help him obtain his freedom, if not, then he asked her to kill him. She then told him that she would not assist in his killing. He looked directly at Adrian, saying, "I thought you would want me dead since I killed your father."

Isabelle grabbed Adrian saying, "He is messing with you because he is scared."

He replied, "Maybe he is, maybe he isn't, either way, he must die." She told him that they should use the cryptid as bait so they could follow him, and maybe he will lead us to the other cryptids or possibly even a demon. He asked her if she would be scared if they encounter a demon, especially since they wanted her dead.

She replied, "I live in constant fear, so unless you have a better idea, then we should go along with my plan. If we do encounter a demon, then at least Raphael is with us." He released his grip on the creature's throat and instructed him to get lost. He warned him that he would kill him the next time they met.

Raphael asked why they had let the cryptid go so willingly. Adrian said, "Isabelle thinks the creature will lead us to where the others are located, but I feel he was sent here to lead us into a trap."

The archangel replied, "Maybe you are correct, but I think we should follow him. We are not picking up any cryptids so far, and we have been searching for two days." Isabelle told both Adrian and Raphael to keep going, and she would take Charlie with her and follow the cryptid. The archangel advised against splitting up, but Adrian agreed it was a good idea. He told them if it appears that the creature was just wandering around, then they should head back.

Charlie replied, "Will do! If we run into any sort of danger, then I will teleport us back to this current location." He gave them his blessing as he and the archangel continued to lead the Lobos. Adrian would eventually find out it was all a trap designed by Ashmead.

After walking for a couple of miles, they finally caught up with the creature. Charlie then looked down at his bracelet and yelled out to Isabelle, warning her there was a demon close by. Before she could even reply, she saw Ashmead standing in front of her. He told her to listen and instructed Charlie to get down on his knees if he wanted to stay alive. The demon told him if Isabelle promised to come back to him, then he would spare his life. She replied, "If my two options are death and being your slave again, then I choose death." Before he could say another word, a second demon appeared and grabbed Ashmead. It was Dagon who had come to put an end to his first-in-command.

Ashmead pleaded with Dagon to let him go because he was bringing Isabelle to him. He told Ashmead that he was pitiful and weak, and just the sight of him disgusted him as he threw him into a demon cage and lit it on fire. Next, he brutally killed the young cryptid by ripping off his arms then swiftly breaking his neck. The king of hell looked at Isabelle and Charlie with fiery red eyes and asked them if they liked his handy work.

He stated he could throw Ashmead in the pits of hell, but watching him burn continuously in his cage was much more rewarding. "Since he helped a cryptid and assisted the Aces in killing Jason, I feel that this is a better punishment than death. What do you think, Mr. Ace?" Before Charlie had an opportunity to reply, the demon grabbed Isabelle and disappeared. Utterly terrified, he looked over at the burning cage, then got up and teleported back to the others.

# Chapter 21

Charlie frantically returned to the location where he had previously left Adrian and the other Lobos. As soon as he arrived, he began running through the woods, screaming at the top of his lungs. A few minutes later, Adrian stopped in his tracks and ordered everyone to start heading back. Raphael said, "Something terrible has happened; I can feel it."

He replied, "Come on, I think I hear Charlie calling out to us." Shortly after, Charlie had finally caught up with the others. He was so frantic he could barely breathe much less talk. Adrian placed his hand on his shoulder and asked his friend to calm down. Please take a minute to collect yourself so you can tell us exactly what has happened.

He replied, "Isabelle and I had caught up with the cryptid when Ashmead greeted us. The demon tried to convince Isabelle to go with him. Before she could reply, Dagon appeared and threw Ashmead in his cage. He lit the cage on fire as he grabbed Isabelle disappearing in a cloud of smoke." Raphael then asked Charlie to please take him to the burning cage. Charlie replied, "Okay, follow me."

As Adrian stayed behind with his people, Charlie took Raphael to see Ashmead. Once they arrived, Raphael could hear the demon screaming in agony. Raphael asked Ashmead if he knew where Dagon had gone and why he had decided to take Isabelle with him. Ashmead told the archangel to go screw himself, saying, he had now lost everything. Jason had betrayed him, Isabelle despised him, and now he was forever trapped burning for all eternity. He was shocked that Dagon had not killed both Isabelle and Charlie, but in reality, he didn't give a shit.

The demon stuck his head through the bars as he asked them why they cared so much about the female bitch or had they just come to watch him burn. Raphael stood right in front of Ashmead, stating, "Your reign of terror is over," as he stabbed him in the face with his dagger. The cage immediately stopped burning, and the demon turned into ash. He looked over at Charlie and told him, "It is time to go. Today is a massive win for us, but not knowing what Dagon is planning next worries me."

The young Ace asked about Isabelle. Raphael replied, "I'm sorry, but she is probably as good as dead."

Once Raphael and Charlie returned, they saw the Lobos under attack. Adrian immediately asked his friend to start teleporting the youngsters out of harm's way. He told Charlie to get in touch with his brother and take the youngsters to him. Adrian and the elders continued fighting the cryptids even though they were hugely outnumbered. After several attempts, he finally talked to Micah. He advised his brother to come and get them instead of sending the youngsters to him. He vanished as he went to get the other Aces. Adrian looked at Raphael, saying, "That kid has a hearing problem. I know it is not in your DNA to kill cryptids, but can you protect and keep the youngsters safe while I fight until help arrives." Raphael then gathered up all the youngsters as he shielded them with his wings.

Seconds later, Micah and the rest of the gang appeared to help even up the odds. Tommy and Mack ran over to assist Adrian and the elders while Micah and Toby stood guard around the kids. Some of the cryptids ran off once reinforcements arrived. Looking around, Adrian said, "I think we killed around a hundred creatures; however, my people had some casualties as well. It would have been worse if the Aces had not arrived when you did."

Charlie replied, "I'm sorry man, I tried to get everyone back as quick as I could."

Adrian told Charlie that there was no need to apologize. He told him right now they needed to burn the bodies, and he would help the elders bury the fallen Lobos. Looking around at all the carnage, Toby asked where Isabelle was. Raphael asked her to sit down while he explained what had happened. After hearing the terrible news, Toby took off running in the direction where Isabelle was last seen. Seeing the pain in her eyes, Tommy took off running behind her. Before Micah could even react, Michael and the other archangels returned.

The hierarchy looked directly at the Aces and said, "We need to talk."

Michael informed everyone that what Victor had told Micah was right, "There is another powerful demon, and his name is Dagon. He is the only fallen angel besides Lucifer that wasn't killed. We believe he is planning something we won't be expecting. The demon has now lost both Ashmead and Jason, so Dagon will most likely be looking for a replacement. He probably left Ashmead burning because he was furious at him for being so weak and for assisting in Jason's death. There are numerous demons he could choose from, but it is anyone's guess who that demon will be. Ashmead had been his first-in-command for over four hundred years. Whoever it is, that demon will probably be more ruthless than Jason and Ashmead combined."

Charlie asked Michael about the cryptids and what Isabelle had told him. He asked if it was true that both Isabelle and Toby must die to end the cryptid race permanently. Michael replied, "Yes, that is correct. Once he turned Isabelle, he had created what is known as 'The Queen' to the cryptids. In theory, if the queen dies, then so do all the others. Ashmead indeed had affection for her, which was why he secured her well-being, but now that she had turned Toby, no one was sure if those same rules still apply. Yes, both women would need to die to eliminate the cryptid race. Isabelle knows that angels can't kill her; Lobo won't kill her because she isn't a threat to them, and demons will forever torture her."

Charlie then asked, "Is that why she asked me to kill her once this is all over."

The archangel replied, "Yes it is, I'm sure she had hoped you or one of the other Aces would end her torturous life. She has wanted to die ever since she was turned centuries ago."

Once everyone had finished burning or burying the numerous bodies, Mack asked if they should go after Toby and Tommy. Micah replied, "No! Toby is upset she just needs time to process everything, plus I'm not worried, Tommy is with her. Right now, we need to figure out what our next move will be."

Michael replied, "Uriel will come back with me while Raphael and Gabriel stay behind to assist the Aces. I feel next time the cryptids attack; they will not be alone. If I am correct, then you will need more than just assistance, you will need help from above."

Adrian looked at Micah and asked if everyone was ready to head out.

He replied, "Yes, we are ready; let's head out, my friend."

Meanwhile, Dagon was back in hell with Isabelle by his side as she asked him how long he planned to keep her chained up next to him. He replied, "Until you agree to follow out my orders and kill Victor and Toby. My patience is wearing thin, so unless you want me to start conflicting pain upon you, then you need to make a decision soon."

She told him that he could kill her for all she cared because she would not hurt anyone. She went on to say to him the Aces would find a way to destroy him. The demon just laughed, "Humans can't hurt me, but nice try. Don't worry, and I will let you choose which Ace dies first. Maybe little Charlie or lover boy Mack, I will give you a day or two to think about it." He told Isabelle that he had someone he needed to see as he threw her ass into one of the demon cages.

After running for several miles, Tommy had finally caught up to his sister. He told her there was nothing she could have possibly done to change the outcome. The only thing that remained was the burnt metal demon cage. The good news was Ashmead is dead, and Isabelle might be alive. She glanced at her brother, saying, "I know you are trying to help, but you hate Isabelle. You don't care if she lives or dies."

He replied, "Yes, I do hate her, but I love you. There is nothing I wouldn't do for you. So please take a few minutes to process everything, and when you are ready, we will go back and re-group with the others."

She kissed her brother on the cheek and told him to give her a few more minutes. She looked around, then sat down next to the cage as she stared at the sky.

# Chapter 22

Meanwhile, in the pits of hell, Dagon met with Lucifer. He asked his master what should he do with Isabelle and if he had any recommendations for his new first-in-command. He glared at Dagon, saying, "If you have to ask for my recommendation, then maybe you are the wrong demon for the job. You should force her to either be your servant or convince one of the Aces to kill her. Jason focused on world domination while Ashmead lost sight of everything due to Isabelle. The question is, what are you focused on?"

The king of hell stated he wanted the Aces to fall by the hands of one of their own. Dagon looked at Lucifer and said, "But first I must find a replacement for Ashmead. I need to find a demon who is vicious but who is also highly intelligent."

Before he could say another word, the devil replied, "Take Lilith as your new first-in command. You should have chosen her when you elected Ashmead." Dagon thanked the devil as he left his presence.

Dagon went to find Lilith so he could convince her to become the next first-in-command. Lilith was a very smart, sneaky, beautiful, and extremely lethal demon. She was currently living in Miami Beach, Florida, where she possessed a young, rich, sexy tycoon's daughter. As soon as she sensed Dagon was near, she demanded he show himself.

He said, "Who are you to command me to do anything. I am the king of hell, and you will follow my lead."

She sat up from her beach chair and pulled down her sunglasses as she replied, "Give me one good reason why I should give up my amazing life and help you. If you took charge of Ashmead years ago, then you wouldn't be in your current situation. I have caused chaos and destruction for over two millenniums, have you forgotten that I was one of Lucifer's first demons. So please sit down and give me your master plan that is if you even have one."

"Of course, I have a plan; with your help, we are going to end the Aces permanently. The first thing we need to do is convince Tommy to join us and turn on his fellow Aces. He already has hate in his heart, and he does not care for angels very much. Then we will kill Isabelle and force Toby to follow while you lead the cryptids."

She looked at Dagon, saying, "No, you have been sitting on the sidelines for decades while Ashmead ran the show. The only thing you were correct about is how hatred is starting to take over Tommy's life. He is a ticking time bomb that I plan to exploit fully. Killing Isabelle would be extremely stupid; let's use her against the Aces. We can start by attacking Victor because technically he should have died years ago." He told Lilith that she knew where to find him once she was ready to start.

A few hours later, Lilith met up with Dagon in hell. She first asked him where he was keeping Isabelle. He walked with her into the next room, where Isabelle was chained to a wall. As soon as Isabelle saw Lilith, she began to get fearful. She asked Lilith why has she come for her after all these years. She looked at Isabelle and said, "I heard you had been a very bad cryptid, so I have come to punish you. Is it true you defied Ashmead and have been helping the Aces and Lobos?"

Isabelle replied, "Why are you asking me questions when you already know the answers. I am tired of being tortured, please just kill me now."

The female demon just laughed and told the cryptid she had come to retrieve her.

Dagon disconnected the chain from the wall and handed it to Lilith, saying, "Do what you wish with her but promise me when the time comes for her to die, be sure she dies a very slow and painful death."

She laughed, saying, "Slow deaths are my specialty."

Lilith told Dagon she would see him soon as she left hell with Isabelle in hand. She first told the cryptid they were off to pay Victor a surprise visit. "He is going to be so excited to see us that he will probably scream himself to death." She told Lilith that she would not help her kill Victor or any other human.

The demon replied, "I don't want to kill anyone either, but since Dagon pulled me away from my sun tanning, I might as well do something fun. Now come on, let's go see him before his shift ends."

Isabelle and Lilith arrived at the base when Lilith killed two of the female guards and took their identification cards. Isabelle said, "There was no reason to kill those women; you are just drawing attention to yourself." She ordered the cryptid to stand behind Victor's desk as she waited behind the door. A few minutes later, Victor rolled into his office.

He asked Isabelle why she was there, but before she could reply, Lilith attacked him from behind. She shut his door and threw him from his wheelchair. She grabbed a bronze award he had sitting on his desk and repeatedly hit him in the face multiple times. Once he stopped moving, the demon took the knife from his uniform and slit his throat. Isabelle tried to stop Lilith but was struck in the back of the head with the award, knocking her out cold. The demon laid Isabelle next to Victor and placed the knife in her hand. Once she saw other soldiers running down the hall, she stood up and vanished.

The MD examined First Lieutenant Richardson and realized he was dead before they had an opportunity to check his pulse. They immediately called his commanding officer Mr. Wade and took the female civilian into custody. Once the Captain came down to the lieutenant's office, he verified that his friend was murdered and was in complete shock when he found out who they had in custody.

He requested to meet with the prisoner alone as he had multiple questions for her. As soon as Isabelle saw Charlie's dad, she stood up and pleaded with him, saying she had nothing to do with Victor's death. He replied, "You are nothing but a monster, why should I believe anything you tell me. I would advise you to get comfortable because you are going to be behind bars for the rest of your miserable life." She begged him to hear her out, but he refused and then walked out of the room.

Mr. Wade went back to his office, and the first thing he did was call his two children. He first spoke to Charlie and told him that he needed to see him immediately and then asked him to hand the phone to Micah. As soon as he said hello, his stepdad told him the same thing. Micah replied, "No problem; we are on our way."

Once they both arrived, the officers escorted them straight to their father's office. Charlie said, "Dad, what is the dire emergency?"

He replied, "Just follow me, I have your friend in custody, and you won't believe what she did."

Charlie and Micah followed their dad to an area of the base they had never seen before. Charlie asked his dad if these were holding cells.

His dad stated, "Yes they are, now please come on; she is down here toward the end."

The two brothers just looked at each other and said, "Who is this person that dad keeps mentioning?" Once they got to the end of the hallway and saw Isabelle, they froze in disbelief.

Charlie's second reaction was, "Thank God, you are still alive; I thought for sure Dagon had killed you."

Micah followed with, "Why do you have blood on your hands, and why are you behind bars?"

Mr. Wade replied, "The military police found her next to Victor's dead body with a knife still in her hand."

Isabelle looked directly at everyone and declared once again that she didn't kill Victor. She informed them it was a demon named Lilith, who is now working with Dagon.

Micah replied, "Who is Lilith, and why should we believe you?"

She said, "After all we have been through if you don't trust me, then I guess it doesn't matter. Lilith is bad news; she makes Ashmead and Jason look like boy scouts. Just think about it, why would I save Toby and fight alongside you guys just to kill a former Ace."

Micah asked his stepdad what will happen to Isabelle. He told them that she would remain locked up until her court date, he then asked them if they believed her. Surprisingly they both replied, "Yes, she is telling the truth, but we have no idea how to prove it."

The boys told their dad to look after Isabelle. They stated, yes she is a cryptid, but she had no reason to hurt anyone. She has never attacked or killed another human being. The only person she has ever bitten is Toby, and that was only because Tommy and I asked her to save her life. Mr. Wade replied, "I can make sure she gets a fair trial, but if she is found guilty, then there is nothing I can do to save her."

They thanked their dad for letting them know about Isabelle and told him they would keep in touch. As the brothers were walking away, they both said, "We need to talk to Michael and get more information about this demon named Lilith. So let's head back, once we retrieve Tommy and Toby we can fill everyone in on the latest development." Isabelle sat back down inside her cell, wishing she could just kill herself. Even though she did not kill Victor, she hated herself none the less.

# Chapter 23

Charlie and Micah arrived back to the others and found that Tommy and Toby had returned as well. Micah informed everyone that Isabelle was alive and well but currently was being detained by his stepdad for allegedly killing Victor. Toby was speechless as she told everyone that there was no way Isabelle could hurt or kill anyone. Charlie replied, "We agree with you, but unless we can prove otherwise, then the United States Navy will prosecute and convict her of murder in the first degree."

Micah added they also had learned there was another demon they needed to worry about, "Isabelle told us this new demon named Lilith is the same demon that took her to the military base and framed her for killing Victor."

Toby replied, "We must do everything humanly possible to help her out of her current situation."

Micah stated to everyone, "Don't worry, we will!"

Raphael requested Michael's presence so the angels could talk to the Aces about Lilith. While they waited, Raphael told stories about how amazing Victor was and all the good he had accomplished. He stated not only was he an outstanding Ace, but he was also one of the best humans he had ever known. He indeed had a selfless heart and would offer to help anyone in need. He probably accomplished more after his accident than before, and that said a lot.

Micah replied, "He helped me to understand the meaning of being an Ace in the small amount of time we had spent together. His memory will never be forgotten, and his legacy will forever carry on through us." Seconds later, Michael and the other archangels returned.

Michael asked everyone to gather around so he could tell them about Lilith. He informed everyone, "She is a very sneaky, brutal, intelligent, and outspoken demon. She is one of Lucifer's favorite demons, and she is also one of the oldest demons in hell. She has been laying low over the past four decades, but don't let her fool you. She is very much involved in everything around her. She has been hanging around South Florida recently before being recruited by Dagon. She currently possesses a rich man's daughter while enjoying celebrity life. If she is Dagon's new first-in-command, then just know she is running the show, not him. The only thing she fears is the devil himself."

The archangel stated that setting up Isabelle for Victor's death was a shot toward the Aces, "She was simply telling us that she is in charge, and she means business. So Aces, please do me a favor and never take Lilith lightly. She makes all the other demons look like precious little angels compared to her. Our focus, in my opinion, should remain the same. We need to be hunting and killing cryptids. The more cryptids we destroy will eventually draw out the demons. As far as Isabelle, she is in the safest possible place she could be right now. Yes, I understand Lilith knows where she is, but going back to the base is risky even for her. Finally, is anyone opposed to my current plan? If not, then let's go, we have a lot to accomplish."

Micah went to gather everyone when he noticed his brother was nowhere to be found. He asked Mack and Tommy if they had seen him, and they said they had not. He then asked Toby if he had mentioned anything to her. She said, "No, but he is still upset about what happened to Isabelle. Maybe he went outside to clear his head."

He replied, "My brother doesn't clear his head, he resolves problems head-on. I hope he is not planning on doing something extremely stupid. We are heading out in the morning, so while everyone is preparing, I will attempt to find Charlie."

Meanwhile, Charlie decided to return to the base so he could help Isabelle escape. Once she saw Charlie had returned, she begged him to leave. Isabelle said, "I appreciate you coming to teleport me out of here, but I will not allow you to become a fugitive. Your dad is a high-ranked official, and if they know you returned to bust me out, then you will be arrested, plus your father will be arrested and dishonorably discharged from the service as well. Do you want that for you and your father?"

He replied, "Of course not, but I don't know what else I can do to help you. Please stop being so brave and just come with me."

She replied, "No, please leave. I will not allow you to throw your life away for me. If you try to teleport me, then I will scream to the top of my lungs right after I bite you. Do you understand me?"

Charlie nodded his head as he looked at her one last time before saying goodbye.

As soon as Charlie arrived back, his brother started to question him. He told Micah to calm down and ensured him that he didn't do anything stupid. He stated he went to check on Isabelle and that she was doing just fine.

Micah replied, "Do you know what could have happened to you or your dad if someone saw you there? One or both of you would be facing disciplinary action so severe that no one would be able to help you."

He told his brother to calm down, and yes, he completely understood the consequences if he had been caught. "Isabelle gave me the same speech as soon as she saw me. Our job is to help people, but what good are we if we can't even help an innocent person who is currently held for a crime she didn't commit."

Micah replied, "I understand that, little brother, but we have to handle this the right way."

Mack walked up to Charlie, saying, "I know how you feel, she is a part of the team and we are held helpless at this time. I am glad you didn't bring her back even though that was your sole purpose of seeing her. We will find a way, just be patient; everything will work itself out."

Charlie replied, "I know! It just pisses me off how demons can cause so much damage. How are we going to be able to prove she didn't kill Victor? It is not like demons can leave behind their DNA."

"Mack told everyone to get ready for the morning. I'm sure we will have more time to brainstorm everything once we get some rest."

The next day, the Aces and angels were back on the trail hunting cryptids. The archangels came along because they feared since Lilith was involved, she would probably release demons with the cryptids. Everyone spent the entire day searching, and by the end of the day, there were no creatures in sight. Micah was starting to get frustrated, and Tommy was already swearing and cursing. Tommy looked at the group and said, "What are we doing out here? It feels like we hunt and kill a handful of cryptids, and if we are lucky, a demon dies too, but will this madness ever end."

Uriel replied, "Be patient, my young friend. Regardless of how much progress we make, it is still progress."

Before he could answer back and call Uriel an idiot, Dagon appeared and took Toby. He looked at his mentor, saying, "Don't just stand there, what are you waiting for? Go after him!"

The archangel replied, "I can't; he took your sister straight to hell."

Tommy took a second to look at everyone as he said, "Screw all of you, I will do this myself!" And he left on his motorcycle. He kept talking to himself as he was riding along. He knew there was no way he could rescue his sister alone, but he knew one person that could help him. Even though he hated Isabelle with all of his heart, he knew she could help him retrieve his sister. He didn't know how he would be able to free her, but he felt he had to use any means necessary. As he was heading toward the base, he had no idea how he was going to bust her out. Once he was about a mile out, he noticed a woman lying on the road. Tommy stopped to assist her, not knowing it was a demon.

He stopped his motorcycle and got off to check on the woman. As soon as he approached her, she stood up and headed straight toward him. He said, "I'm guessing you are

Lilith, and you came to kill me. Let's dance because I promise you I will not go down without a fight."

The demon replied, "Killing another Ace this week would be amazing, but if I wanted you dead, you would be. I thought we could talk about your sister instead. You must be extremely desperate to come here. What makes you so sure Isabelle will help you even if you are successful at busting her out?"

Tommy told her the only thing that mattered right now was saving his sister. So he gave Lilith two options: leave now or kill him.

She began to laugh while saying, "I like you, how about I give you a third option? You can either break Isabelle out and possibly get killed, or you can walk with me, and I will give you exactly what you desire most."

He left his bike on the side of the road as he began walking with Lilith. She told him that he had a lot of hatred in his heart and was currently fighting his own demons within, so if you think about it, we have a lot in common. She asked him if he saw himself walking away from this war. He replied, "I care about myself and my family only. My question to you is, why am I wasting my time; it is not like you will release my sister."

The demon asked him, "After everyone you have lost, and with your incredible powers, why do you continue to take orders from Micah and the archangels? If you join me and turn your back on them, then you will become the ultimate Ace, and then there will be nothing standing in your way. All your so-called friends wanted Derek dead, allowed your sister to be attacked, and never stood beside you while you grieved your mother. In my opinion, the Aces and angels are assholes, not your friends."

After listening to everything she told him, he replied, "Let me guess, my sister dies unless I decide to help you."

Lilith told him, no, this was an invitation, not a trade. She told him that she is a brutal demon who loves to be in control, but she is also a demon who allows people to make their own choices. "If you want to be free, then this is the route you should take. The bottom line is, all Aces eventually die, then they get replaced with new recruits who are eager to save the world. Do you want to be just another statistic or something greater?"

The demon told Tommy to think about what she had told him, and when the time comes, he can make his own decision. Lilith also told him as a token of faith; she would give him something until they meet again. Before he could reply, the demon was gone, and his sister appeared. Being lost for words, Tommy grabbed Toby as he refused to let her go. She looked up at him, saying, "I don't understand what just happened, but I am very thankful to see you, brother."

He replied, "Me too," as he walked her over to his motorcycle.

# Chapter 24

When Tommy and Toby returned, the first thing Micah asked was how he was able to rescue his sister from the demons? He told everyone that he was heading toward the base to break Isabelle free when all of a sudden, Toby appeared out of nowhere. Michael looked at Tommy, saying, "That makes absolutely no sense whatsoever."

Toby replied, "The only thing I know for sure is Dagon took me to hell, and a female demon brought me back. I am assuming that the demon was Lilith, but she didn't say a single word to me. One second I was in hell and the next I'm standing in the street staring at my brother."

Michael told everyone that there had to be more to the story because Lilith would not do anything without reason.

Micah replied, "Yes, I'm sure there is more to this story, but right now, let's be glad that Toby is alive and well."

Michael pulled the other angels aside and asked them if they had eyes on Tommy while he was gone. All three archangels stated no, they were out searching for Lilith instead. With an irritating look, he instructed Uriel to .remain by Tommy's side. The hierarchy was worried that a demon had encountered Tommy and had made a deal with him. He told his fellow angels he believed that was how

Tommy was able to bring Toby back. The demon wouldn't just release her without a motive. There is more to Tommy's story than we probably will ever know.

Meanwhile, Dagon requested his demons go find Lilith because he needed to talk to her. He sent three demons to search for her and informed them not to return until they located her. Later that afternoon, Lilith appeared in front of Dagon and asked him why he had her summoned. He began yelling at her and asked why the hell she had let Toby go.

She replied, "First of all, you are truly a dumbass. Second, no one tells me what to do except Lucifer, and finally, you attract what you want with compassion, not anger. You want Tommy to help us eventually; then you have to befriend him first." She told him, "The disgruntled Ace doesn't care about anything or anyone except his sister. So I delivered her to him out of good faith. Trust me; my plan is going to work; you just need to be patient."

As she left his presence, Dagon started to destroy everything around him out of pure rage. He slaughtered numerous demons and repeatedly screamed, saying, "I hate Lilith, I truly despise her down to my soul. I don't understand why the devil favors her over me. It makes absolutely no sense, especially since I have stood beside him ever since the fall." He thought to himself if her plan doesn't work, then he may need to kill Lilith. He would not allow another demon to do whatever they want under his watch. He tossed the worthless demons he had killed in the pits of hell as he was on a mission to find Michael. What better way to hurt both Lilith and Tommy simultaneously than informing the archangel of some fake news?

Dagon appeared in the surrounding area where the Aces and archangel were currently located. Mack told everyone that his bracelet had picked up a demon nearby. Michael asked the others to keep everyone safe while he checked to see who was lurking in the woods. The archangel walked about a hundred yards through the forest when he noticed Dagon sitting on a stump. He told the demon that he wouldn't be hurting or taking anyone this evening. The demon replied, "I'm not here to capture anyone. I came to talk directly to you. Do you want to hear what I have to say? If so, shut up and listen because I will only tell you once."

Michael instructed him to go ahead. Dagon informed the angel that he had taken Toby to hell with him, and then Lilith came and brought her to Tommy. She first requested to use him as a vessel, which he declined, then she promised to hand over Toby if he promised to turn on his fellow Aces when the time came.

Michael replied, "You know I don't believe anything you say. You are nothing more than a bitter fallen angel."

Shaking his head, he told the hierarchy to believe what he wants but don't say he wasn't warned. Before Michael could reply, Dagon was gone.

Michael went back to camp and grabbed Tommy by the arm and ordered him to tell everyone what had happened. Being completely livid at his remarks, Tommy hit Michael directly in the chest. He told the archangel never to lay hands on him again. He swore to his sister and everyone else that he did not make any kind of deal with Lilith. "She told me that one day all the Aces would burn in my presence, and there will not be a damn thing I can do about it. She returned my sister as a reward for killing Jason. She thought it was amazing that a human had killed a demon. She informed me that no man in history had ever destroyed one before me. So next time a demon tells you something about me, make sure it's true first. Oh, that is right; Dagon was once an angel, so he must be a 'righteous' demon. Sorry, I forgot my bad!"

Micah pulled Tommy aside and told him he had no right to strike an angel. He just looked at his friend and said, "Wow! Thank you for showing me your true colors. I guess being your friend since grade school means absolutely nothing compared to a heavenly angel. My question to you is simple: Do you believe your precious guardian angel or me? You don't even deserve to date my sister. The one time she gets hurt was under your watch, but if I retrieve her and bring her back safely then I must be working with the enemy."

Micah replied, "I didn't say I don't believe you, I just said you had no right to strike Michael. His approach to questioning you was wrong, but your reaction didn't make things better. If you say you didn't make any deals with Lilith, then I believe you, end of discussion."

Tommy glared at his friend as he said, "I got your back along with the other Aces, but for all I care, the archangels can kiss my ass."

Adrian walked up to Mack and Charlie to ask when they would be heading back out to hunt for cryptids. He told them if they planned to wait until morning, then he planned to take the Lobos and leave tonight.

Mack replied, "Don't you think we should stay together? We are much stronger as a unit. Every time you leave us, your people are attacked, and you lose more members of your family."

Adrian told the guys, "Since everyone is so hostile right now; my people don't need to get involved with your drama. We will head out tonight, and I will keep Charlie updated."

Before the Lobos left that evening, Adrian asked Charlie to relay a message to Isabelle. He told his friend to let her know he had her back, and she had earned his trust as well. He replied, "Aww.... Lobos do have a heart, and don't worry; I won't tell anyone."

Adrian and the elders headed out with all the youngsters and continued going south. Charlie reminded him once more, "If you encounter any trouble at all, then you call me, and we will be there."

He replied, "Yes, I know, thank you again, my friend. You better do the same, and please keep an eye on Tommy; he is very uneasy right now."

Charlie replied, "He is always a hothead. Once he blows off some stream, he is usually fine afterward."

Adrian led the youngsters upfront while the elders followed behind in the rear. He told his most trusted advisor, "Some of these kids are stronger and faster than us, why did my father always hold the youngsters back so much?"

He replied, "Your father wanted the youngsters to be innocent for as long as possible. We didn't choose this life; the angels chose for us. Even though I was your father's best friend and advisor, I must say he would have been proud to see the great man you have become."

What Adrian didn't realize was Lilith was watching them very closely in the distance. She was sizing them up in her head as she recognized the Lobos were more of an ally to the Aces than she first realized. She was debating whether or not to attack them but understood she needed to remain patient. The goal was to follow the plan she and Dagon had designed in their heads. She knew when this was all said and done; the Lobos would cease to exist. Lilith thought to herself, *If I can't convince any of the Lobos to help me, then I will create a division among them.* As her evil mind was spinning, she began to laugh uncontrollably. Once the Lobos heard a noise in the distance, she decided to vanish among the moonlight.

Lilith returned to hell to inform Dagon that her plan was starting to take shape. She told him that Tommy's blood was beginning to boil, and it would only be a matter of time before he planned another strike on the angels or even his fellow Aces. The Lobos had separated themselves again and were now hunting alone. The archangels were focused on Tommy and had let their guard down. Isabelle is locked up and my personal favorite, the Aces have no clue that their lives are slowly crashing in on them. She gave a sly look as she said, "Now, do you see my plan is smarter and better than yours?"

Dagon replied, "Don't get carried away just yet. It is too soon to know how this will play out for us and the cryptids. But so far, I'm impressed."

# Chapter 25

Back at the military base, Captain Wade was working with his superiors and the attorneys' to get a hearing date for Isabelle. He told the officers he wanted to talk to her in private. The military police advised against it, saying, "She is extremely dangerous. We don't know what she is, but it's not human."

He replied, "I will be just fine; please go find us a secured room to use."

Ten minutes later, they returned and escorted the prisoner down the hallway so the Captain could talk to her. Once they entered the room, the Captain explained there were no recording devices in the room, and this was the safest place for them to talk. If you trust my sons, then just know you can trust me too.

Captain Wade told Isabelle that he knew about her and the supernatural world. He went on to say he knew for over two hundred years she had bitten only one human. He also knew that the one human she did bite, she did because Micah begged her to save Toby's life, which you did without any hesitation. He also told her it was hard for him to imagine she would attack and kill Victor in cold blood after all these years. He said, "I believe you are innocent just like my children do, but is there any way to prove that a demon killed my friend?"

Isabelle replied, "No, demons are like ghosts that hide in the dark. If a demon possesses someone like Jason did, then you could pin it to that particular individual even though it wasn't really them. The problem with that is Lilith burns the fingerprints off of every vessel she inhabits. So the question is, did your officers find any strings of hair that wasn't mine. Once a human is possessed, then they no longer bleed. If an individual stabs a possessed person, then he or she would die, not from bleeding out but from them losing their soul."

Captain Wade said, "So I need to check and review the evidence for any hair particles."

She replied, "Yes, that would be a good start. However, if you find any, then the next question is, how would a person capture Lilith. She would most likely kill your soldiers or abandon her vessel if we even tried to approach her."

"He told her they have to at least try for Victor's sake. We can't stop her, but if we have a body, then we can at least have a dead suspect and a closed case. Now let's get you an attorney and back behind bars."

She replied, "Why do you care what happens to me?" He told her that he always stands behind his family and their friends.

The next day, Isabelle appeared in front of the judge where she pleaded Not Guilty to first-degree murder. The judge asked if the court needed to appoint her an attorney. She said, "No, your honor, I will represent myself. I understand it is risky going into a murder trial and not have representation, but this is my fight and my life on the line." Captain Wade was sitting in the back, just shaking his head from her response. He couldn't believe she had turned down legal representation. He knew it was a poor choice on her behalf, but couldn't say anything in front of the judge.

Afterward, he pulled Isabelle aside and said, "I hope you know what you are doing, especially since you turned down having counsel. I will do my part and check the evidence room, but you are now on your own."

She replied, "I appreciate you trying to help me, but you owe me nothing. I now see where Charlie inherited his kind heart and compassionate soul from. I can see you raised both your boys the right way."

While Mr. Wade was heading to the evidence room, he decided to call his son Charlie. He told him that his friend stood in front of a judge today and refused counsel, and a trial date was set for early next month. He asked his dad if she had any chances of beating her murder charge. Mr. Wade told his son, "It would take a miracle to find Isabelle not guilty. Don't forget, she was found over Victor's body with the murder weapon in her hand."

He informed his son that he would go over all the evidence again, but once the trial started, it wouldn't last very long. "It is bad PR to have a murder on base and not charge someone with the crime in a reasonable amount of time. We like to keep stuff out of the media coverage as much as possible." Before ending the call, he warned his son that if he came to revisit Isabelle, then he would arrest him for trespassing. "If someone sees you teleport in and out of the base, then the military will turn you into their personal lab rat." Charlie apologized to his dad as he hung up the phone.

Charlie informed the other Aces and archangels that a trial date had been set for Isabelle. He told everyone that her chances didn't look good, but they hopefully had time to change her fate. Tommy told everyone that they needed to focus on killing cryptids, and eventually, the sorry ass demons would show their faces.

"Let Captain Wade keep doing his job, and we will continue doing our job," Michael replied. "Tommy is right; we must keep moving forward. I do feel for Isabelle, but her current situation is not our main focus right now."

Micah stated, "We should have left last night with Adrian and his people; we keep making ourselves vulnerable every time we split and separate."

Toby replied, "I agree with both Micah and Tommy. We need to head out tonight, so we will only be a day out from the Lobos. It is going to take all of us to win this war."

As everyone was preparing to head out, the group had a surprise visit from one of the youngsters. He told everyone that after the Lobos left last night, Adrian instructed him to head back to inform them they were heading back to ground zero. Micah asked what the youngster's name was, and he replied, "My name is Jacob, I'm Adrian's brother." He asked the young Lobo why his brother decided to return to their home.

He told the Aces, "There is no need to fight until his people are forced into battle. My brother is starting to understand why our father led the way he did for so many years. My father wanted to keep everyone safe, and ever since Adrian has guided us, we have lost too many of our own. Just in the past few months, we have witnessed two-thirds of our people killed by either demons or cryptids. It is starting to take a tow on Adrian, but he did state he will be ready to fight when the time comes."

Charlie asked Jacob if he was going to stay, or was he just here to relay the message. He told everyone that he would stay until it was time to rejoin his people.

As everyone was preparing to head out, Charlie received a call from his mom. Mrs. Wade was worried and wanted to know how everyone was doing. He told his mom that they were managing and prepared to head out and do more hunting. She informed her son that she heard about his stunt at the base. She warned him how dangerous that would have been if he had carried out his plan. Charlie promised his mom that he wouldn't do anything stupid, and he was very aware of the outcome if he had busted Isabelle out. He said, "Mom, sometimes when you aren't thinking clearly, you start doing some dumb shit. Thankfully, it was Isabelle who convinced me to leave before I made everything worse. I apologized to dad, but as I told him, I just wanted to help my friend."

She replied, "I understand, but sometimes you can't help everyone. It scares me that you and Micah are these supernatural beings, but I couldn't be more proud of both of you. Promise me one thing. Please stay alive; I won't be able to handle it if I have to mourn you or your brother." He promised his mom that they would be safe and stay together as he told her goodbye.

Micah told his brother to hurry up since everyone was waiting on him. He informed Charlie that he was talking to their mom while waiting for him to finish packing his bag.

He looked back at Micah and asked, "Did you know Adrian had a younger brother?"

He replied, "I had absolutely no idea! I thought he was an only child, and that is why he favored you so much."

As he walked away, Charlie threw his bag at his brother, calling him an irritating ass.

"Come on, man, I'm just messing with you. There is one request I need to ask of you."

Charlie said, "Shoot, what do you need?"

Micah asked his brother if he would stay with Jacob because he would hate to tell Adrian something had happened to his baby brother.

He replied, "No problem, consider it already done."

Michael told everyone they first needed to start searching around town. He stated he had a feeling that the demons would bring the fight to them, and they would have all the cryptids with them when they came. Mack replied, "Sounds perfect. Hopefully, we can end the madness shortly because I'm so tired of constantly looking behind my back."

Tommy glanced over at Mack and informed him, "The madness will never end. The battle between good and evil has been going on since the beginning of time. We will come and go, and if we die, then the archangels will just recruit a new Ace. Look at Victor, do you honestly believe our outcome will not be any different than his?"

Uriel pulled Tommy aside and asked him to tone it down a bit and that everyone there had the same goal. So if they worked together, then anything was possible. Tommy told his guardian angel that he quit listening to him shortly after meeting him. Toby grabbed her brother and told Uriel to please not pay any attention to him. She told the angel that her brother had been moody since birth.

# Chapter 26

Back at ground zero, the place Adrian called home for him and his people. The Lobos were working on fixing their land and rebuilding their homes since it was destroyed months ago. The elders were upset because after they had abandoned their home, the demons and cryptids had come through and destroyed their personal property. One of the elders asked to speak to Adrian alone. He asked him why he had sent Jacob away and then decided to return to their old home.

Adrian said, "First of all, this is not our old home; it is our birthright. Second, I wanted to keep my brother safe because one day, he will become the next leader of our people, and finally, once the war starts, the youngsters will remain here."

The advisor replied, "So it will just be you and all the elders that will fight."

Adrian told him that he would let each of the elders decide for themselves if they want to fight or not. "The war is not our top priority. Keeping our legacy alive is and will always be our primary focus."

A few of the elders took watch as Adrian, and the youngsters cleaned up the mess left behind from the invasion. Most of the personal property was destroyed, but the foundations of their homes were solid. The top advisor asked Adrian why he wanted to rebuild instead of finding new land to establish as their new home. He replied, "I'm doing what my father would have done if he was in this same scenario. We shouldn't have to start over or run and hide. Lobos are proud people, and we need to show that same mentality to the younger generation so that they can carry it on to the next. One day my brother will rule over us, and he will look at me as his advisor. If I don't lead by my father's example now, then neither will he when the time comes." Adrian continued, "My brother is more of a leader than me. I feel like my focus should be helping and protecting both Lobos and humans."

The advisor replied, "The Aces are rubbing off on you. I just hope they are not clouding your judgment." He gave the advisor a dirty look as he walked away.

The elder was afraid Adrian was losing his edge and started to question all of his decisions. He did like and respect Delisle but was feeling trapped living in isolation. He didn't like how Adrian was aggressive and wanted to fight until the last cryptid was dead. He also wanted their people to be free and have the opportunity to live independently, just like humans. In his opinion, their old life and homes were destroyed, and a fresh start is what they needed. He wanted to tell Adrian his thoughts, but Lobos were always taught not to question their King. In the past, such offenses were penalized by death or exile from the group.

Challenging the King had only occurred twice since the elder was born. The first person was the King's first advisor who Delisle, sentenced to death, and the second person was his son Adrian.

Meanwhile, Lilith was still lingering around the Lobo camp, observing their attempt to rebuild. She thought to herself, *What are they doing? Don't they realize that cryptids or demons can attack them at any time?* Wanting to understand, she decided to follow the elder, but once he realized a demon was tailing him, he immediately transformed into a werewolf. She looked directly at him, saying, "I respect your bravery, but you can't be that stupid to attack me. I could kill you within a matter of seconds, so please don't test me."

He decided to charge the demon regardless as he was prepared to die, and it could be today. He would slightly sink his teeth in her at least once before she snapped his neck.

Once he charged Lilith, she responded by tossing him up against a pine tree. She said, "I didn't realize the elders were so stupid, I thought elders were wise and knowledgeable advisors. Would you like to try that again because you are doing a fantastic job of entertaining me right now?"

He stood up and growled as he charged her yet again. This time she caught him in mid-air and proceeded to choke him. Right before he passed out from lack of oxygen, she loosened her grip as the Lobo fell to the ground. She had her foot on his throat as she gave him a proposal. She told him if he would help her kill Adrian, then he would rule the Lobos, and the demons would let them live in peace.

He replied, "No! I will never betray my people. I rather die first."

She smiled as she stated, "Death works for me, too," as she stomped his face into the ground until his body was no longer moving.

Looking down, she said, "Damn! This asshole caused me to get blood all over my new shoes, and now I smell like a wet dog." She then took his dead body and tossed it into the river.

After a while, Adrian was getting concerned that his most trusted advisor had not returned. He instructed several of the youngsters to go out and search for him. The youngsters went out and searched everywhere, but once they smelled blood, they immediately stopped in their tracks. One of them questioned their next move, "Should we keep searching, or is it best to head back and inform Adrian?"

Before the guys could decide, Lilith appeared in front of the boys. Saying, "Oh look, little cubs! Are the three of you as dumb as your old stupid advisor?"

As the youngsters went to escape, the demon grabbed two of them as she ripped off their heads. The lone Lobo just stood there in fear as he didn't know what to do next. She informed him that she would allow him to live for now because she needed him to deliver a message to Adrian.

She said, "The end is near, and when the time comes, you will be defeated by your allies."

As she watched him run off, she stated, "Wow, that was fun!"

Once the kid returned to ground zero, he could barely breathe or even talk. Adrian asked him what had happened and where the other two were. The youngster replied, "We encountered a demon, and she killed your top advisor and my friends. Lilith spared my life only because she wanted me to relay a message to you. She stated that your allies would defeat you before the final battle is over."

Adrian shook his head in disbelief as he ordered the youngster to continue working while he visited with the remaining advisors. The advisors all looked at Adrian, saying, "Today is another great loss for us all. First, we lose our King, and now we have suffered the loss of perhaps the greatest elder of all time. We need to stop rebuilding our lives and fight before our people are no longer in existence." He stated their position would stay the same for now, but once the battle started, he planned to fight until the very end.

The advisors walked away, thinking their King had betrayed them and their people. They wanted to overthrow Adrian but didn't know if Jacob was ready or even capable of taking over as the King. The biggest concern was trying to stay alive, but they were beginning to think death would become their outcome. One of them stated that if they could eliminate all the cryptids, then maybe, just maybe they could be free. They believed it was time for them to be free and no longer under the services of the archangels.

Until recently, demons had never really interfered in their lives. The new top advisor said, "It is our partnership with the Aces that has made us enemies with the demons. Let's assist everyone by getting our homes rebuilt; then, we can convince Adrian to continue hunting again."

One of them asked, "What if he still doesn't want us to hunt."

The top advisor replied, "Then we all need to make a choice and do what we think is best."

Lilith sat back from a distance and thought how easy it would be just to invade their camp and kill everyone right now. However, that wasn't part of her master plan. She was patiently waiting and plotting, so when the time came, everything would unfold in their favor. The goal wasn't to kill everyone because that would be too easy and not much fun. What the demons wanted was to see the Aces and Lobos crippled to the point they lose all hope.

Lilith's thought that was much worse than losing or dying, just thinking about it, put a massive grin on her face. She started to laugh uncontrollably as she said to herself, "The Aces and Lobos are so screwed, and the best part is they will never see any of this coming. I love knowing that my plans always work, unlike Dagon's stupid small-minded ideas. One day soon, hell will have a new ruler, and that individual will be me, not Dagon because sometimes the best man for the job is a WOMAN!"

# Chapter 27

Lilith decided to leave the Lobos alone for now and go check in on the Aces. She knew they were becoming impatient and were preparing to head out soon. The last thing the Aces wanted was to wait for trouble to find them. So she decided to have some fun by releasing a group of newborns their way. She enjoyed watching the 'good guys' fight; she thought the Aces were cute, especially Charlie. There was work to do before Tommy would be ready to join her voluntarily. A few more encounters with some cryptids should do the job before we start invading the military base and permanently ending this war.

While Micah was leading everyone out, he started a conversation with Mack. He asked Mack if he thought Tommy would betray them at some point. He said, "I'm torn. On the one hand, angels are not capable of lying, and also, Tommy is our friend."

Mack replied, "I guess anything is possible. I mean, look at all the crazy things we have encountered already in the past few months. My opinion about Tommy is he is our best friend so that I will put my faith in him over the angels."

He asked Micah to think about where the archangels were getting their information. "The intel came from demons, and they are nothing more than lying, evil, chaotic, and manipulative pieces of shit, so Tommy would have to show me something before you can convince me that he is a traitor."

Micah agreed by saying, "I feel the demons are trying to separate and pin us against each other. We must remember we are more than just friends; we are family."

Tommy was talking to Uriel, asking him if he could use his mind control on cryptids since they were part human.

Uriel told him, "Using that particular power is extremely dangerous. Were you not listening to me while I was training you?"

He said, "Yes, of course, I was listening. All I'm saying is why can't I use my mind control and have them kill each other."

The archangel replied, "Besides being dangerous, it is also tricking other creatures into murdering each other. If we kill them in self-defense, that's one thing, but tricking them into killing each other is another. We should never murder anyone for fun, nor should you ever abuse your powers. Cryptids are still partially human, and our job is to protect the human race. Would you like to talk about something else because this topic is over?"

Tommy replied, "No, I'm good. You are right. Let's focus on the mission at hand."

Toby was following behind Tommy and Micah because she wanted the opportunity to get to know Jacob when Charlie asked her why she was walking with them instead of her boyfriend or brother.

She said, "I wanted to talk to Jacob, plus I'm here to keep you safe. You know cryptids and demons can attack us from any angle."

Charlie replied, "Very funny, I don't need your protection; I am a grown-ass man."

Toby laughed as she told him yes, you are all grown up, but we are still very young, especially Jacob. The young Lobo spoke up and asked if they thought they needed to babysit him because they were friends with his brother. Toby said, "No, I have seen you in action. You are truly a badass! I just want to know why Adrian never informed us that you were related to him."

He replied, "Probably for the same reason he does anything which is to protect the people he cares about the most."

"Well that sounds good to me, how about you, Charlie; do you have any more questions for the youngster?"

Charlie shook his head as he told Toby to return to the front and check on their brothers.

"We have everything under control here, but thanks for asking, I appreciate you." She blew Charlie a kiss as she left to talk with Micah.

She walked next to Micah and grabbed his hand, asking very playfully if he had missed her. He replied, "We are all on the same path; what are you talking about."

Toby looked at him, saying, "Yes, I know that, Mr. Genius. I was trying to be cute and sweet with you."

He replied, "Yes, sweetheart, I understand that and I appreciate it very much, but right now, we should be focused and not flirting with each other."

She jumped in front of him and demanded he kiss her before taking another step forward. Trying not to get frustrated or mad, he leaned over and kissed her. She replied, "No, I want a real kiss; show me how much you love me." He looked around and saw that everyone was staring back at him.

Mack said, "You better listen to her, or we won't get anywhere, which will force us to make camp right here."

A second later, Tommy chimed in, "Just kiss my damn sister already before I punch you in the face. We don't have time for this game you are playing; we are preparing for war." Micah grabbed her and drew her near, planting a passionate kiss on her lips. She looked at him while stating that it was much better, now we can proceed.

Toby continued walking with Micah while asking if she had embarrassed him. He told her that she could never embarrass him, but right now was not the right time to be flirting. She replied, "I wasn't flirting, I just wanted a kiss from the love of my life. Doing what we do, I never know if our last kiss will be our final kiss, so you can't fault me for wanting to kiss you every opportunity I get."

He leaned over and kissed her again, saying, "I understand, but I'm not planning on any of us dying any time soon. We will all be victorious once this is all said and done."

He asked Toby if she would trade places with her brother, saying he wanted to talk with Tommy, plus it looked like the archangels were aggravating him once again. She kissed Micah on the cheek as she walked back to fetch her brother.

Tommy caught up with Micah, asking him if he was going to give him another lecture on how to talk or treat the archangels. He said, "I wanted to talk to you about what our game plan will be when everything escalates. I don't want any of us to die or end up in a wheelchair like Victor, so do you have any suggestions?"

Tommy replied, "I know this is selfish, but I don't want anything to happen to Toby or my father. I have suffered too much loss already, but that doesn't answer your question."

He told his friend that he understood because he made it his job to keep everyone safe. He apologized once again for failing to keep his sister safe.

Tommy said, "I am no longer mad at you because of what happened to Toby. I am not sure what Mack's outlook is about this battle we will soon be involved in, but if he is not willing to fight to the death, then he needs to go home. We both have loved ones we don't want to lose. His parents, however, are elderly and have recently retired and are currently safe and enjoying life down in Key West, Florida."

Micah told Tommy, "Even though Mack did not have any relatives in the surrounding area did not mean he was not invested in the upcoming battle. If you are correct and I am wrong, then maybe it's for the best that Charlie gets Toby, Mack, and Jacob to safety while we stay back and fight."

Tommy replied, "Yes, I agree. I would rather die than experience the loss of my sister, and I'm sure you feel the same about your sibling. So are you saying just you and I will fight this war?"

Micah replied, "I don't know what the right call should be. I just don't want to lose anyone I care about once this is all said and done. We can try to convince the others to leave if things go wrong, but you know, just like me, they won't listen to us."

"Maybe you are right, Micah, but we won't know that until it happens."

Mack told Toby that Micah and Tommy were probably talking about them and how it was their job to keep everyone safe. "You are probably correct, but they don't make decisions for us, we do," Toby said. "I'm sure Micah told Charlie to keep Jacob safe and told you to keep both of them safe. Just like they are telling each other to make sure they keep me safe. Does all of that sound about right to you?"

Mack replied, "Yes, it does, but you can't blame them for wanting to protect their siblings. The reality is we might not all survive this battle, so it's good that we are not naïve about our chances. If the archangels do their part and the Lobos come through when we need them, then our chances are better than you realize."

Mack nodded his head, "Hopefully, you are correct, but that doesn't mean I'm not scared."

She replied, "Me too, but that is what makes us human. Our will to live outweighs our odds, and that is why I have never lost faith." She put her arms around him and reassured him that everyone was in this battle together till the very end.

Before she could say anything else, she noticed Mack's bracelet lighting up. She yelled out to everyone that they were about to receive some unwelcome guests. Micah looked down and saw his and Tommy's wrist bands lighting up yellow. He called out to Charlie, telling him to get Jacob to safety. The young Lobo informed Charlie not to teleport them away because he was eager and ready to fight. However, Charlie grabbed him before he could even finish his sentence. He took him to the only place he knew he would be completely safe, and that place was home.

Jacob ripped away from him, yelling and screaming, "What the hell is your problem. Now they are down two capable people who can help kill cryptids."

He replied, "My order was to get you to safety if anything happened. I would rather teleport you against your will than watch you die or even worse telling Adrian something happened to you."

Adrian and the elders came out as soon as they heard Jacob's voice. Charlie told his friend that he had to get back but would fill them in later. Adrian embraced his brother and waved to Charlie as he returned.

The archangels created a barrier entrapping the Aces and the cryptids together as they fought each other. They couldn't get involved unless they witnessed one of the Aces in danger or if a demon became involved. Tommy ran over to help his sister while Mack fought beside Micah. Toby was like a wild beast attacking and ripping the heads off any cryptid she could get her hands on while her brother was giving her added protection.

She yelled at her brother, telling him that she didn't need his help. He replied, "You might be more experienced than these newborns, but they are much faster than you. Plus, I am stronger than you and all the other cryptids combined. Don't look at it as help; look at it as me giving you an added assist."

She just rolled her eyes as she said, "Whatever brother, if that helps you sleep better at night, then we will go with your stupid logic."

"Thanks, sis, I love you too. Let's finish this playful bickering after we are finished killing all these bastards."

As the Aces were slowly killing off all the cryptids, Lilith ordered a new demon to go and attack one of the archangels. She promised him a promotion among her army if he hurt or destroyed one of them. This particular demon was young and very stupid and had no idea he was walking into a death trap. The demon attacked and went straight for the wings of one of the archangels. Michael saw the demon out of the corner of his eye as he turned around and snatched him.

Raphael looked over and saw how this demon wasn't necessarily bright as he took out his dagger and stabbed it through the demon's chest. Gabriel asked why one puny insignificant demon would even dare try to attack four angels' much less four archangels. Michael replied, "I'm sure it was Lilith. She wanted to see if we were paying attention, but at least now we are down one more demon."

A few minutes later, the attack was over, and all the cryptids were dead. Micah asked what that crazy uncoordinated attack was about. Michael replied, "It was a test. So be prepared, the worst is yet to come."

# Chapter 28

Once everyone regrouped, they all stated it was probably best for them to stay close to home, anticipating the battle would be heading their way. Michael replied, "Oh, this is just the teaser; the demons will be releasing their army of cryptids very soon." Micah asked Charlie to retrieve Adrian and the other Lobos and have them return because the battle would soon be underway. Charlie left immediately and teleported back to ground zero, so he could request his friend's assistance. He never expected there would be some friction among the Lobos once he arrived.

The elders told Adrian it was time to fight, and if they survived this war, then it would be time for them to go their separate ways. He told his advisors he was the king, and he did not take orders from anyone. His new top advisor informed him they had voted, and all agreed that after the battle, Jacob would be the newly appointed king. As he was about to attack his advisor, Jacob and Charlie grabbed hold of Adrian.

He turned around and said, "Did you know about this, brother. Or were you the one planning this all day?"

His brother replied, "Are you kidding me? do you even have to ask such a ridiculous question? This is all their doing, and you know what brother, the advisors are pissing me off too. I know I'm not fit to be the king I'm merely just trying to stay alive and help our people."

Charlie looked at everyone as he said, "This is not the time to be fighting among each other. Either you want to help us, or you can stay right here, but choose quickly because I'm not waiting around."

The elders replied, "Go ahead and go; we will come once the battle begins."

Some of the youngsters stayed behind with the elders while the majority of them went with Adrian and Jacob. Charlie started teleporting all of the youngsters first. As he was going back and forth with the Lobos, Adrian said to his brother, "I am glad you did not side with the elders. I try my hardest every day to be the best possible leader I can be for our people. I understand the elders want me to do more and be less like my father, but that's impossible because I am my father's son."

Jacob replied, "You know I will always stand beside you no matter what happens. Not only did our father raise us to do the right thing, but so did our loving mother. You are trying to keep our father's tradition alive, which is excellent, but you must lead us your way, not his. We both know the elders were way out of line for even questioning you. If you want to be mad at them, then fine, I understand, but this is not the time."

Adrian put his arm around his brother and asked him when did he become so wise. Jacob smiled, "Since the day I started walking in my brother's footsteps."

Meanwhile, Toby asked if someone would go with her to visit Isabelle. Michael asked why it was so important to go right now. She replied, "Isn't she the key to this war? I mean, our goal is to stop the demons and kill all the cryptids, but their goal is to make sure that Isabelle and I are well protected. The last thing the demons want is for us to die because if that occurs, the entire cryptid population would be extinct. She informed everyone that Lilith would torture us until one of us agreed to help her. Once that occurs, what will stop her from killing the other?"

Tommy replied, "Lilith will not dare try to kill you, I guarantee it. Let's go; I will go to the base with you."

Michael just glared at Tommy, telling him to be careful and to stop being so cocky.

He stated he wasn't cocky, but extremely confident, "You see, I still have one good functioning hand, and I will gladly lose it to kill Lilith if it means protecting my sister."

Micah instructed both of them to go to the base and ask for Captain Wade. Toby kissed Micah on the cheek as she left with her brother.

Michael looked at Micah and said, "Your friend is getting more and more nonchalant regarding the demons. He thinks just because he killed one and Lilith just released Toby to him that he knows them better than we do. The demons will destroy him before he even sees it coming if he doesn't get his act together."

Micah replied, "I agree he can get extremely cocky at times, but trust me, Tommy is no fool. He knows how dangerous the demons are and how important the results of this battle will be, not just for us but for the entire population. So please stop worrying about him, Toby will make sure her brother doesn't do anything stupid that would jeopardize the others."

Once Toby and Tommy arrived at the base, she asked her brother if she could speak to Isabelle alone. He first stated that it was not safe when she quickly responded, "I am not asking, I'm telling you to please wait at the gate for me. Please trust me to do this without you."

He stated it was not about trust; it was about losing her.

She said, "I understand that, brother, but just ride around for an hour, then circle back and come get me."

Against his better judgment, he agreed to let her see Isabelle alone. He told her if she was not at the gate when he returned, then he was coming in to get her.

She replied, "Try not to do anything stupid as I know you would hate it if your sister had to come and rescue you."

Toby walked up to the gate and requested a meeting with Captain Wade. The officer called over to his office, and when he answered, he ordered them to let her in. He instructed one of the officers to drive her to the back of the base where they held the prisoners. The officer dropped her off as the Captain granted her permission into the restricted area. He asked Toby why she decided to see Isabelle now. He told Toby that her trial was set to begin next Monday at 09:00. She told Captain Wade how she thought Victor's murder involving Isabelle was a setup and part of their master plan.

He replied, "Are you telling me that the creatures are planning to attack this base?"

She told him not only to attack it but kill everyone in the process, including Isabelle.

Meanwhile, as Tommy was riding his motorcycle, he noticed a woman standing in the middle of the road. He pulled off to the side and noticed it was Lilith. He asked her if he should start praying since she was there to kill him. She replied, "No silly, you are my favorite, but have you given any thought to our recent conversation? I know your fellow Aces will try to destroy the cryptids, and if they do, that means bye-bye to your sister and best friend."

Yelling at her, he said, "Isabelle is NOT my friend. My sister is off-limits, and I will do anything to keep her safe."

Lilith told Tommy that she was not the enemy, "Once the battle begins, my demons will be watching over and protecting Isabelle and Toby. What will your friends be doing?"

She said, "Just think about my generous offer. Help me, and I will make sure no one ever hurts your precious sister, or you could help your friends and watch your sister die. The choice is yours, but remember in the heat of the battle when you see me wink that will be your cue to make your final decision. Now head back and get your sister, you don't want to keep her waiting."

As Tommy was heading back to the base, his head was spinning with all the possible conclusions that could occur from this battle. He knew the only people important to him were his father and sister. He wasn't worried about dying, but he would die inside if he ever lost Toby. Tommy had mixed emotions about his friends, and he was starting to build up a hatred for the archangels. He thought maybe Victor was right, and the end game for the Aces was eventual death, and there was no escaping it. He kept telling himself there was no way his best friends could kill his sister even though it would end the cryptids. He wasn't quite sure about Adrian and the other Lobos, but he was confident Micah would never allow it to happen. Once Tommy arrived to pick up his sister, he knew he was ready to do whatever was necessary to keep her safe.

Toby walked out of the gates with a giant smile on her face. She told her brother she was glad to see him and reminded him that she wasn't late. He told her to stop bragging and get on the bike before he left her. She asked if he enjoyed his ride and he replied, "It was great, there were no signs of any cryptids, which made me sad, I was hoping to find one to kill."

She asked why he couldn't just ride and enjoy the scenery. He stated, "That would be boring, besides I'm a hunter. I feel out of place if I am not killing."

She shook her head as she said, "What am I going to do with you? You are probably more stubborn and hard-headed than all the Aces combined."

He just laughed, "Thanks, sis, love you too! Let's stop and have some lunch before we head back; I'm starving." She put her arms around her brother as she instructed him to hit the road.

# Chapter 29

While the archangels were preparing the Aces and Lobos for the upcoming battle, Lilith was busy lining everything up so she could witness the fall of the Aces. She had Tommy exactly where she wanted him. There was still some work to be done with the elders, but she knew eventually they would understand what needed to be done. She knew if Tommy decided to betray his friends and the elders ended up turning on their king, then her job was done.

Next, she started going back and forth, gathering up all the cryptids, telling them they had two choices: they could assist the demons, or she could kill them now and be done with it. Some of the cryptids did resist, but the majority of them decided to follow her instructions. One of the cryptids said, "She is more ruthless than all the other demons combined."

Lilith replied, "I sure am little one. Come walk with me; you are now my favorite."

As she was gathering all the cryptids, she wondered what Dagon was currently plotting. She knew she needed to see him before they started their attacks, and she was hoping he was preparing as well, but she would not be surprised if he were not. She thought to herself, *If everything goes as planned, maybe Lucifer will allow her to run hell and not Dagon.* She knew the devil was pleased with her work, along with how he had always appreciated her loyalty to him.

Lilith was excited to be back in the game and felt once everything was said and done, she would become the first queen of hell. She thought to herself; *It has been way too long since someone with balls has ruled over hell.* Ashmead had some in the beginning, and Dagon had lost his edge centuries ago. The only demon, in her opinion, who had ever taken charge, was Jason, but unfortunately, he was always too low on the food chain to make any kind of noise. She loved his enthusiasm, but he never really had an end game. Lilith instructed the cryptids to continue heading toward the base, and she would catch up to them; eventually, there were a couple of pit stops she needed to make first.

Lilith's next stop was at ground zero because she wanted to check in with the new elder advisor. Once she saw him out in the woods, she decided to approach him while no one else was around. She asked him if he had made a decision since their last discussion.

He replied, "No, I have not. I don't think Adrian is fit to be our leader, but turning on my people just feels wrong."

She got up in his face telling him the next time their paths crossed, he better have an answer for her. "You help me, and I allow some of your people to live, or you can defy me and watch everyone die. It's your choice, old man, but remember you better choose wisely for the sake of your people."

Meanwhile, in hell, Dagon was busy watching and observing Lilith's every move. He was starting to wonder how long it would take for her to arrange this master plan of hers, or was she just out playing and becoming reckless. He knew Lilith had a hidden agenda; he just wasn't sure what it was. Dagon missed the days before Lobos and Aces. He said, "Those were the good old days when we just tempted and possessed humans. Every once in a while, we would kill a human or angel, but to us, it was more fun just to cause chaos and destruction. Maybe if we destroy the Aces for good, the archangels will stop anointing recruits every generation." He knew it was wishful thinking, but would God allow the archangels to continue appointing humans with extraordinary abilities if it meant they would perish. Dagon was willing to see how this battle played itself out because he never gets his hands dirty unless it is necessary.

Dagon became impatient while waiting on Lilith to return, so he decided it was time to go and see for himself if she and the cryptids were prepared to attack the military base. Once he arrived, he asked her if this was all of the cryptids. Lilith replied, "Yes, it is, minus the ones I was forced to kill because of their disobedience."

He looked at her with pure disgust in his eyes. He informed Lilith it was idiotic for her to get rid of their hired hands. Instead, she should have forced them to fight with us, not kill them. He looked at her and said, "Have you always been this stupid or has the promotion gone to your head?"

Being extremely pissed off at his harsh words, Lilith decided to walk away instead of lashing back at Dagon.

He continued to speak to her as she walked the other way, "Once you realize that I'm in charge and not you, your life will become so much better."

Very pleased with himself, Dagon asked all the cryptids to circle around him so he could inform them they would be attacking a military base in less than forty-eight hours. Their only goal was to kill all the Lobos, and if they succeeded, then they could focus their attention on the Aces. He told them not to worry about the archangels because he planned on having his demons keep them busy. He promised the cryptids if they were successful in killing all the Lobos and each of the Aces, then he would release them from his command.

One of the cryptids spoke up and asked Dagon why they should believe him. He said, "That is an excellent question. I admire your spirit and your stupidity, I can't determine which one I like the most, but you definitely have a set of balls! To prove to all of you that this is not a trick, I will go ahead and release the cryptid who spoke up for all of you." The young cryptid nodded his head as he turned around and started to head the other way. After he left, Dagon ordered one of his demons to go kill him once he was ultimately out of sight.

Next, he knew he needed to talk with Lilith again, hoping she had taken some time to cool down. Dagon realized she was a hothead, but nevertheless, Lilith someone essential to his cause. Once Dagon reached Lilith, she asked him what he had promised to the cryptids to get them in agreement.

He said, "I promised the one thing that every trapped individual wants to hear. I told them if they are successful at killing all the Lobos and Aces, then I would release them."

She replied, "Let me guess, one of them challenged you, so you granted his freedom but then later ordered a demon to go kill him."

He laughed and said, "Wow! You know me so well, I'm honored. So now that you are caught up to speed, are you ready to help me get started? The plan is to attack the base early tomorrow morning."

Lilith replied, "Of course I'm ready, you idiot. Who do you think has been aligning and making sure everything is in place. I'm not the one who has been lying around doing nothing for the past few weeks."

Dagon looked at her and said, "Let's go we need to give everyone their instructions, I will disregard your idiot remark."

Dagon and Lilith both returned to where the cryptids were, but first, they made a pit stop in hell so Dagon could summon more of his demons. She replied, "You know they are not your demons, and if Lucifer thinks you are abusing your power, he will take it away. Would you have even chosen me to be your first-in-command if Lucifer didn't get involved and encourage you to do so?"

He replied, "Yes, I would have regardless. Because you were the best possible option. Now can we move forward, or do you still want to debate with me?"

"No, we need to gather as many demons as possible because morning will be here before we know it."

Once the king of hell had his army of demons, everyone was set and ready to go. Dagon told everyone to be prepared to attack at dawn. Dagon instructed the demons to draw the archangels toward the outside perimeter. He asked the cryptids to keep the Aces busy within, telling them to be ready to fight to the death once the battle began. "If any of you try to quit, I will kill you. Now, if everyone ends up following my instructions, then two things will occur. A majority of us will not perish, and we will finally be free from the Lobos and Aces."

Dagon looked at Lilith and said, "If your master plan does fail, you will never see the light of day ever again. Not only will you be forced to stay in hell, but I will make sure you rot the rest of your days within your demon cage."

She mumbled under her breathe, "You can run your mouth, for now, Dagon, but once I am victorious, you will become my little bitch."

The next morning, Dagon asked Lilith to lead everyone toward the base. Most of the demons surrounded the perimeter of the base while the majority of the cryptids breached and went onto the grounds. As soon as the alarms sounded, one of the MP notified Captain Wade and informed him they were under attack. He instructed them to secure the prisoner and start getting everyone to the underground bunker.

The MP stated, "You want us to flee instead of fight. We are the United States Navy. We don't run and hide; we fight and protect our country."

Captain Wade replied, "Yes, I would agree if this was a terrorist attack, but we are no match to confront supernatural beings and demons. Just please do what I have ordered you to do, I am on my way."

As Captain Wade ran out of the house, he yelled to his wife to contact the boys and tell them we need some back-up immediately. Mrs. Wade grabbed for her phone as she dialed Micah's number. Hearing his phone ring, Micah reached across the nightstand and answered it quickly once he saw it was his mom. In a very frantic voice, she started to yell, "You and the archangels need to get to the base RIGHT NOW! They are under attack. Your stepdad is already in route, please be safe and make sure all three of you come home to me."

He replied, "We will, mom, just promise me that you will stay there until this is all over. Love you, mom, I will see you again."

As soon as Micah hung up the phone, he rushed to wake the others because he knew every second counted. Michael instructed the other archangels to start teleporting the Lobos to the base. He warned everyone to be careful and informed them that they were in for the fight of their lives.

Adrian helped his brother get all the Lobos prepared as Jacob transformed and took some of them on foot. Once his little brother had left, Adrian yelled to Mack and asked him if he was ready. Mack replied, "Yes sir, I'm ready to kick some ass. Grab your warrior swords because Charlie is ready to take us."

Micah told Charlie to head out, and he would be right behind him.

Once everyone had left, Micah looked at both Tommy and Toby, saying, "This is what we trained for, ready or not here we go." Toby stood between Micah and Tommy and grabbed each of their hands as Michael teleported them to the base.

# Chapter 30

Once all the Aces arrived, Michael asked Charlie to get everyone onto the base, including his dad. He and the other archangels would stay outside fighting off the demons. Toby looked at Charlie and said, "Get me inside, and I will find Isabelle."

After he teleported Tommy and Toby inside, he went back for Micah and his dad. As soon as Toby was within the walls, she took off running toward the holding cells while killing as many cryptids she could along the way. After fighting through dozens of cryptids, she finally made her way to Isabelle.

She looked at her friend and said, "Come on, it's time to get you out of here." Isabelle told her they could either run and hide or stay and fight, but the overall outcome would not be in their favor.

Toby replied, "Regardless of our odds, I'm here to fight, care to join me?" Toby took the keys from one of the dead officers and released her friend.

Adrian called out to his brother and told him that some of the Lobos needed to go outside and fight. He informed him the cryptids were flooding in by the dozens, and if they didn't stop them halfway, then they would overpower them.

Jacob yelled, "Stay inside and help the Aces, and I will start the charge outside to help reduce the numbers." Before Adrian could even reply, his brother and dozens of Lobos were already out the door. He quickly realized that even though he was worried about his brother, he knew he had to focus on the creatures inside the walls. He yelled out to Mack for some much-needed assistance.

Mack replied, "I am trying to make my way to you. Hang in there; these creatures are everywhere."

As soon as Micah and his family were on the base, Mr. Wade ordered Charlie to get all military personnel to safety. He replied, "Dad, I need to stay here and help; we are stronger together." Micah told Charlie that their dad was right. He needed to get as many people as possible to safety. All these soldiers were caught in the middle, and none of them deserve to die.

Micah instructed his stepdad to begin gathering his men so Charlie could teleport them somewhere safe. He told everyone, "Protecting humans and keeping them alive is our top priority. Fighting and killing cryptids is our second priority, but staying alive is their final agenda. If we all manage to walk away after today, then it would indeed be a miracle."

Charlie was getting everyone to safety as fast as his father was gathering the men together. He instructed everyone to run as far as possible before calling for help. One of the soldiers said, "We don't take orders from you, so you better stand down, or we will make sure you are arrested and lock you up for endangering our lives."

Charlie replied, "Go ahead, arrest me, even though I just saved your life. If not, then shut the fuck up and listen.

These creatures and demons will kill you, and they will smile at you while doing it. Any more questions before we move forward." The soldier stopped talking and started to lead everyone far away from the base.

Toby and Isabelle fought their way to the central part of the base, where they finally met up with Tommy, Micah, Adrian, and Mack. The girls yelled out and asked about the others. Micah replied, "My stepdad and brother are working on getting all the military personnel to a safe location. Jacob took a group outside to help cut off the cryptids from flooding the inside while the archangels dealt with the demons."

Isabelle told the group she was heading outside to provide more assistance to the Lobos. Toby replied, "No, please don't, stay here with us! Once the demons spot you, then you are as good as dead." Isabelle glanced back at her friend and told her; one of us has to die, and today is not your day. As Isabelle ran toward the exit gate, Micah grabbed Toby so she couldn't run after her. She asked him to let her go, and before he could reply, Tommy made her promise to stay by their side. Knowing there was no reasoning with them, she promised to fight next to Micah and Tommy.

Meanwhile, Lilith appeared in front of the head elder and asked him if he had made his decision. He then told her to go straight to hell. She shook her head as if she was disappointed with his answer, and without saying a word, she jumped on his back and ripped his head clean off. Before the angels could respond, Lilith had disappeared once again. As Michael looked around for her, he saw Dagon in the corner of his eye. Without thinking, he took off after the first-in-command, hoping to end him permanently. Once Lilith noticed that Michael was pre-occupied, she used that as her cue to sneak onto the base.

As she was making her way in, she was intercepted by Isabelle. The demon just looked at her as if she had lost her mind. "Are you seriously trying to challenge me?"

Isabelle replied, "If you want in, then you will have to go through me. So whatever you do, don't underestimate me."

Once Lilith heard her run her mouth, she decided to charge at her. Isabelle dodged her and bit the back of her neck as she threw her down to the ground. She then stomped her face multiple times as Lilith just laid there laughing, asking her if that is all she had to offer. She went to stomp her again, but this time Lilith caught her foot and snapped her ankle in half. Isabelle fell to the ground screaming not able to get up.

Lilith then reached down and grabbed a rod off the ground and was about to put the rod through her chest when Isabelle leaped up on one leg and pushed her through a window breaking the glass. Lilith brushed the broken glass off as she again grabbed the rod this time, stabbing it right through Isabelle's chest, who then looked at Lilith telling her to finish the job. Lilith then picked up a piece of the broken glass and halfway slit Isabelle's throat.

She looked down at the Queen Cryptid and said, "I could cut your head clean off, but it is more fun watching you bleed out and gasp for air. Don't worry; this is not goodbye. I will still see your sorry ass again once I finish up here and return to hell."

As the guys were busy fighting and killing cryptids, they stumbled across a bomb that was located in one of the hangers. Micah yelled out to the guys and told them they had another problem to worry about at this time. Tommy and Toby ran over to where Micah was standing and noticed that the bomb was active, and the timer was currently counting down. Micah called his stepdad, hoping he was still alive.

He answered his phone and said, "This better be important because I'm trying not to die here." He told his stepdad that there was a bomb and asked him what they should do.

He replied, "Well, if it's around the hanger, then you have another problem as well. There is ammo, fuel, and other chemicals in or around that hanger. The mixture of everything plus the impact of the blast will level the base and kill everyone nearby."

He told his stepdad to continue helping Charlie get everyone to safety and not to come back to the base for them. Micah ended the call before Mr. Wade had an opportunity to reply back.

Seconds later, Lilith made her way inside where the Aces were and grabbed Toby. As soon as Tommy felt her presence, he went after her telling her to let his sister go. She looked at him and just laughed, saying she didn't want to hurt his sister, because she thought of her like family too. The demon then asked if he had decided on what she previously asked him. He informed her that he disliked everyone but not enough to help her.

She then very angrily said, "Your friends will die; it is up to you if your sister dies as well. If you destroy the Aces, then I give you my word, your sister's life will be spared."

Tommy pleaded with Lilith to let his sister go. He told her that he would do anything she asked as long as she didn't harm Toby.

Lilith replied, "I don't want you to do whatever I ask, I want you to do what you feel is right. Don't make this entire ordeal about me; you know I have been upfront and honest with you since the beginning. Can you say the same thing about the archangels and your so-called friends?"

He put his head down, and once he lifted his head, he said, "You are so right, the Aces must die. Get my sister out of here, and I will take care of the rest."

Toby yelled, "Tommy, please don't do this, she is messing with your head. Micah, Mack, and Charlie are your friends."

Before she could say another word, Lilith disappeared with the precious cryptid.

Tommy came running back in as he told Micah that Toby was safe and currently under the protection of Uriel. He asked the other Aces if they had any ideas on how to disarm the bomb. Tommy asked if Micah could put a force field around the bomb while he looked to see if he could stop the timer by cutting one of the wires.

Mack yelled, "I don't think you should be messing with any of the wires. You could cause it to go off even sooner." Adrian seconded the motion. Feeling extremely stressed, Micah told everyone that unless they had a better idea, then he was going to go forward with Tommy's plan. "Please everyone just shut up, out of all of us he is the only one with experience in wiring and electronics." He told his friend to give him a minute while he made a call. Tommy replied, "You better hurry; we have less than three minutes."

Micah pulled his phone out and called his brother. He told Charlie to go ahead and get Jacob and the Lobos to safety along with their father. Charlie asked Micah why he sounded so worried.

He said, "It's nothing, we have a way to stop this, so please just listen to me."

Charlie replied, "Okay, but as soon as I start teleporting Lobos to safety, more cryptids will start to head your way."

He told Charlie, "That's fine; let them come we are ready. Now stop wasting time and go. Your number one priority is to keep everyone safe." Micah hung up the phone and told everyone to get prepared.

Adrian and Mack got themselves in position to kill any cryptids that came their way. Micah looked at Tommy and said, "Are you ready? Remember, don't touch or cut anything unless you are a hundred percent certain it's the right call."

He told Micah to stop talking and do his job because they were down to ninety seconds. After looking at it for a few seconds, he stated, "I think I got it, lower your force field."

As soon as he said that, several demons came flying in. Mack yelled, "Oh shit, bomb or no bomb. I don't think we are making it out alive."

As soon as he said that, a demon grabbed all four guys. Micah told Tommy to smash the bomb with his fist since everyone was going to die anyway.

Tommy replied, "I'm not going anywhere, but you are most definitely correct. The three of you are scheduled to die today." He looked at his friends with black eyes as he cut the red wire. The timer counted down faster as sixty seconds turned into ten. As the timer was about to hit zero, Dagon appeared and teleported Tommy to safety. As he vanished, he told his friends goodbye.

Immediately after the bomb exploded, most of the base was destroyed and left everything buried in ashes. The archangels rushed to where the hanger was and started to search for survivors. Raphael looked at Michael and asked him to stop because the Aces were gone. The hierarchy blamed himself when he realized it was all a distraction so that he would be caught off guard.

Seconds later, Charlie appeared and asked where his brother and friends were. Gabriel put his arm around Charlie and said, "I am so sorry, my friend, but Mack, Adrian, Tommy, and your brother perished in the explosion. They were trying to disarm the bomb but were trapped between it and several demons when the bomb went off."

Charlie replied, "No, there must be something you can do. The four of you are archangels for crying out loud!"

Michael said, "I'm so sorry, my friend, but what's done is done."

Bursting into tears, Charlie dropped to his knees as he screamed, "NO! I'm so sorry I failed you, brother!"

**End of Book One**